Rob Starr

J. A. Howard

ISBN: 978-1-7356703-0-0 (paperback)
ISBN: 978-1-7356703-1-7 (ebook)

Contents

Letter to Reader,

Before you start this, you should know one important thing, this book is NOT for adults. It's not a charming adventure story or a teen romance (with or without vampires) or a story about some amazing kid who bravely survived a war, or famine, or poverty. It's a story about high school and not even one of those books where things work out if you're a "good" kid or if you do the right thing. Adults will hate it.

They would rather believe – even though they did stupid shit in high school, that somehow – it's changed. They think they are better parents – smarter or "cooler" – than their parents were. They really think all the messages about inclusion and anti-bullying and "no means no" and all the rest of it, have made things easier. But that's not really true. Is it?

This is the story of me, and a boy named Rob Starr. It's only been a year or so since it all happened, so I still remember everything – all the details. Not that I could forget. And I am going to try to tell you the truth – the real, painful, humiliating, sickening, life-changing truth. I am going to do my best to put everything in it, even the stuff that no one talks about, even the stuff that's totally personal, totally mortifying; the bad decisions, the lying, the stupidity, and the selfishness. And I'm going to swear and tell you about the first time I had sex and the first time I got wasted and a whole bunch of other things that are probably going to freak people out; but I don't care. Because the truth is, I did that stuff (and still do some of it) and because I believe that all the things we try to hide from our parents and from each other really only ends up making us feel separate and different and alone.

I'm hoping that maybe, if I'm completely honest about what happened to me, maybe you won't make same stupid decisions

I made. Maybe you won't hurt people you really care about to please people who don't really care about you. And maybe you won't let a boy, even a really beautiful, popular boy, make you feel worthless.

Maybe not – but it's worth a shot.

Ellsworth High School Case #1141
Transcript of interview: March 21
Student: Mia Morgan
Counselor: Dr. Janis Dubrovski

Dr. Dubrovski: *Mia, before we get started, I want to be clear that this interview is to gather information regarding the events that took place on the night of February 21st. Anything you say here will be held in strict confidence unless we mutually agree that it should be otherwise. Do you understand?*

Mia Morgan: *Yes.*

Dr. Dubrovski: *And for the record, can you confirm you are having this conversation voluntarily at the school's request?*

Mia Morgan: *Yes.*

Dr. Dubrovski: *We appreciate your cooperation here, Mia. Nothing like this has ever happened at Ellsworth before and we're hoping that what we learn from this interview will help us to prevent another incident like this from occurring. That's why we need you to tell the truth to the best of your ability. (pause) This is being recorded for security purposes. Please say okay if you understand.*

Mia Morgan: *Okay.*

Dr. Dubrovski: *Great... good. So..., I know this is difficult, but I must ask you. (pause) Were you raped at Reynold Prince's home on the night of February 21st?*

CHAPTER 1

A Misfortune and a Miracle

October 14th & 15th

I stayed home from school on Tuesday despite the fact that I, Mia Morgan, a short-ish, somewhat geeky, snarky, not-half-bad-at-art and pretty-good-at-math sophomore was virtually invisible. You see, I hung out with the kids no one pays that much attention to; theater-music nerds mostly. We thought we were sort of alternative – we refused to listen to K-pop or top twenty stuff – but, the truth is, we were basically mainstream about everything else. Don't get me wrong, I wasn't a total troll or anything, but I didn't have gorgeously straight hair or a big butt or long legs with perfect thigh gap. I was just one of those sophomore girls who wasn't particularly interesting in any way that mattered.

Like most fifteen-year-olds, although invisible most of the time, I was also painfully visible when I least wanted to be. In other words, even though no one really knew I was alive or took any notice of me – at least no one of any significance – there was still no way I could go to school with something as hideous as a giant zit on my nose. Because when you're fifteen and in that bland center of the pack, people don't notice you *until* you have a disgusting pustule on your face. In fact, it is a guarantee of instant notoriety. It is that very day that you will – for some inexplicable reason – be required to sit next to the super annoying Joey Ricciardelli (or whatever you call this brand of asshole at your school) who could almost be cute if his features weren't so small and close together and his nose hairs didn't stick out in sharp little points. Joey will, of course, take one glance at you and loudly announce to the entire homeroom that Mia Morgan has a huge, bubbling zit on her face, which is just exactly the type of comment that would spark the evil genius of someone like Clark Johnson (one of those guys in your grade who no one really likes but is popular anyway because he's a Sophomore on the varsity lacrosse team) to invent the name Mamma Mia Pizza Face and then, that's it, for the rest of your life.

So, home is where I stayed – just me, my zit, and my TV – which is how I heard about the accident before everyone else. I wouldn't even have seen it because I was watching back-to-back reruns of Teen Mom, but eventually changed the channel because honestly, that show gets really depressing. I mean why do they keep going back to the nasty, lowlife guys that got them pregnant in the first place? Anyway, completely by chance, and because I wasn't paying much attention, I switched to some kind of local news report about an accident: Madeline Gerber-Starr had been hit by a car in the Target parking lot after having bent down to pick up some organic, environmentally-friendly laundry detergent, that had fallen out of her shopping cart.

If you're not from Ellsworth, the town in Westchester County, New York, where I live, then it's hard to convey just how huge a piece of news this was. Mrs. Gerber-Starr was the closest thing we had to a celebrity. This was partly because the Starrs were rich and partly because she was, without question, the hottest mom in our town – always in tight, pastel-colored yoga pants with sunglasses on her head holding back her honey blond hair. It was also understood that – before marrying Mr. Starr – she'd dated some famous New York Yankee or maybe it was one of the Giants – I don't know for sure, but I do know that he showed up at their Fourth of July barbeque one summer and everyone just about lost their minds. But more important than any of this (at least to us kids) was that Madeline Gerber-Starr was the mother of the most gorgeous and most popular boy in our school – Rob Starr, or "Rock" as he was nicknamed by his adoring basketball teammates and fans.

Everyone loved Rob – even me, or maybe especially me – though I would never admit it. If asked, I always shrugged and said he was just like all the other jocks – totally full of himself – but really, deep down, I knew he wasn't. You see, my parents had been friends with the Starrs since we moved to Ellsworth. My mom and Mrs. Gerber-Starr were on every club committee together, and my dad and Mr. Starr had been playing paddle tennis together for as long as I could remember. When we were younger, my little sister Hallie and I spent our summers hanging out in the Starr's backyard pool. The Starrs had three kids: Robbie – that's what we called Rob back then – who was two years older than me; Jake who was my age; and Rachel, who was and still is Hallie's best friend and who has slept over our house at least once a week since the first weekend they met.

Robbie…Rob and I weren't friends or anything like that, but back then he was the kind of kid who was always nice to littler kids; patient and funny, willing to play Marco Polo or hide and seek if we asked him enough times. And he stayed nice. He sometimes even said hi to me in the hall at school which sounds like a perfectly normal, human thing to do when you've known someone for like, ten years, but, well, you know how it is. If you are an incredibly popular senior guy you don't go around saying hi to geeky sophomore girls no matter how long you've known them, except of course, if you're Rob Starr.

As soon as I heard the news of Mrs. Gerber-Starr's accident I ran to the kitchen and pulled up the local news channel on my mother's laptop. My mother was making soup or something. "Feeling better I see," she said sarcastically.

"Something happened to Mrs. Gerber-Starr," I replied and then, there it was on the screen as if my words had summoned it: the police cars, ambulance, reporters.

I don't really remember what happened next except that my mother went into action. She was just that way – born to organize. My sister and I called her Command Central Calista because she always had some project going; a picnic for The Newcomers Committee, the Senior League's Spring Fling, a fundraiser for the MGS (More Green Spaces) group she ran. So, when the accident happened to her "closest and dearest friend," it was no surprise that our house became the motherboard of all activity.

Mrs. Gerber-Starr's accident turned out to be huge deal. She ended up being in the hospital for months: first a coma, then later, when she came out of it, a series of operations followed by more months of physical therapy. Of course, we didn't know anything about all that yet. All anyone knew that Tuesday was that Rob Starr's mother had been hit by a car, which, everyone agreed, was nearly impossible to believe because Mrs. G-S was one of those perfect people – smooth and untouchable – the kind of person that nothing bad could ever happen to. It was obviously very sad, too, although at the time I don't remember feeling sad. I don't remember feeling much at all for Mrs. Gerber-Starr. That probably sounds pretty awful, but I'm trying to be really honest here. And the truth was nothing bad had ever happened to me or even to anyone I knew very well. I had no idea what it all really meant or how I was supposed to feel. So, I certainly wasn't expecting what happened next.

For starters, the Starr kids moved in. Yup, you read that correctly. Rob Starr moved into *my* house. At first it was just supposed to be a couple of nights. Mr. Starr, Bill, was some kind of super successful businessman who traveled all the time. So, when the accident happened, he wasn't even home. He was in India on some hotel development deal. With Mrs. G-S in the hospital, it only made sense (according to my mom) that they move in with us until Mr. Starr could get back to New York and deal with things. That meant Rachel moved in with Hallie (of course, she practically lived in there anyway), I moved into the guest room, and Rob and Jake took my room because I still had babyish twin beds (complete with butterfly bedspreads – ugh). I ran around like a lunatic that afternoon getting all my personal stuff together; I certainly couldn't let Rob see my tampons or zit medicine or the Harry Potter wands that my friend Stephanie and I had made out of chopsticks in the fourth grade.

I didn't see Rob that first day. All the Starrs were at the hospital and got back really late. They were all still asleep when I left for school the next morning – the zit on my nose still pretty brutal looking, having popped – thank the zit gods – but now red and raw and almost impossible to cover without it looking like I'd stuck a piece of pie crust to my face. Luckily for me (and my zit), by the time I got home, the Starrs were gone again, back at the hospital, and so it went for a couple more days. I started to think I was never going to actually see them. But then, on Friday, the first of three miracles occurred.

I got home from band practice at around four – the flute if you must know – and they were all there, sitting at the kitchen table, Rob, Jake, Rachel, and Mr. Starr. They looked surprised when I walked in, as if I had interrupted them in their kitchen rather than in mine. I could feel my face turning red. Just being near Rob Starr made me nervous.

"Um...hello Hallie. Nice to see you again," said Mr. Starr.

"Dad, that's Mia," Jake said, his tone a blend of disgust and embarrassment.

"Of course, it is. Sorry Mia," Mr. Starr said pleasantly though his face was gray with exhaustion. "It's been quite a while."

I nodded and produced what I hoped was a sympathetic smile in return. Then I just stood there not knowing what to do with myself. I was hungry, but I didn't feel comfortable throwing my backpack on the table and boiling up some ramen noodles as I often did after school. Besides, I didn't want Rob to see me eat anything for fear he might think that someone who looked like me – and by that, I mean not in shape – should not be eating ramen noodles or anything at all for that matter. Oh, I know that sounds messed up. I mean it is messed up. I should have just gone ahead and eaten something if I was hungry – but it's not as simple as all that.

You see, the reality is, that most of the girls I know (and I'm guessing most of the girls I don't know) worry about how they look just about all the time. This ends up meaning that most of us are obsessed with food in some way. Not that every girl is anorexic or bulimic or anything. It's just that once you get to a certain age – the age when you start to notice guys (or girls or both), you also realize that having a good body is *really* important. I wish it wasn't true. I wish I could say that it didn't matter – or that I believed that boys would like me for the real me once they got to know me – and maybe that actually happens to some people somewhere on earth – or so my mom insists – but I'm trying to tell the truth here and the truth is, that it's not how it works. Sure, having a good personality matters but how is anyone going to know you have one if they never talk to you.

If you don't believe me, just look around. The proof is everywhere. Take Hermione Granger for instance. In the first three Harry Potter books she's not that cute – big teeth, totally frizzed out hair. But, in book four, Madam Pomfrey conveniently fixes her teeth right before the Yule ball which is, of course, right about the time that they're all hitting puberty because, hey, how could we possibly believe that Viktor Krum or even Ron Weasley would want some brainy, big-toothed, frizzy-haired girl? And let's not overlook the serious double standard here, because let's face it, Ron wasn't exactly boy band material, was he?

And to top it off, in the movies Hermione is played by Emma freakin' Watson from day one. Oh sure, they messed up her hair a little for the first one, but she was basically completely adorable from the start. The point is that the standards are set. And because of it, for most of us, every day there's a little war going on in our minds. Our child brains want ice cream and pizza but our growing up brains want to look good in our jeans and be popular with boys.

I should stop here and say that most of the girls I know aren't disastrously overweight or even close to it. And not one of them is ugly. Every one of us is attractive in our own way. But I promise you, most of us don't think so. I know we're supposed to be beyond this stuff. We're supposed to "love ourselves the way that we are" and "embrace our curves" or whatever the slogans say, but it's just not that easy. When you're constantly subjected to a steady stream of images; perfect girls and women online and on TV, you can't help but think you should look that way too.

Anyway, I left the Starrs in my kitchen with all our food and went upstairs to the guest room to do my homework. By time suppertime rolled around I was famished. With no other choice, I headed back downstairs to see what was for dinner and was surprised to find the kitchen abandoned. A note from my mother scribbled on the message board said she and Hallie had gone to the hospital with the

Starrs and that my dad was meeting them there, and could I order up something for everyone and charge it to her credit card.

At first, I panicked. How was I supposed to know what to get the Starrs for dinner? But then I remembered we'd seen them coming out of China Village one night a month or two ago, and I figured that was as good as anything else. Still, I was left with the dilemma of what to order. I couldn't imagine the Starrs ate the ordinary Chinese stuff (Moo Shu Chicken and Cold Sesame Noodles) that we Morgan's did. I suspected they chose the exotic dishes with names I couldn't pronounce or maybe, knowing Madeline Gerber-Starr, they only got healthy stuff – steamed chicken and broccoli with brown rice. Finally, I just dialed and asked Li, the China Village lady to recommend a mix of things. And that's when the first miracle occurred. When I explained to Li that I needed a big order because the Starrs were staying with us, it turned out, like everyone in town, she knew of Mrs. Gerber-Starr's accident. Not only did she know their usual order, she sent everything over for free! I set the table and the food arrived right on time, just minutes before everyone got back from the hospital.

This probably doesn't strike you as miraculous, but I assure it was. It was because it was the first time Rob noticed me. Not that he saw me standing near the egg rolls and thought 'wow who's the babe holding the packet of hot mustard' but he did notice me. In fact, he spoke directly to me. He said: "This looks great, Mia. Thanks." and I said, "No problem," and he said, "I love Kung Pao Chicken," and I said "Yeah, me too," even though I had never had it before.

I barely ate anything after that despite my former hunger because at this point, I actually wasn't hungry – maybe for the first time in my life. I kept trying to look at Rob without getting caught. He even looked good chewing which, in my opinion, most people don't. It was the way the back of his jaw flexed.

CHAPTER 2

Two More

October 16th – 19th

The second miracle happened about an hour later and at first it didn't seem like a miracle at all. It was one of those times that parents think they're handling things well and they're actually screwing things up. After dinner, which I didn't eat – I know I've already mentioned this but, hey, it was a big deal for me – my parents and Mr. Starr asked us all into the living room. They were casual about it, but somehow it still seemed like they might be about to tell us some really bad news. Apparently, I wasn't the only one who thought so because Rachel started to cry, and I think Jake did too, but he tried to act like he wasn't. Then Mr. Starr had to quickly explain that all he wanted to tell us was that they had decided that the kids should "stay put" for a while since Mr. Starr had to be at work and the hospital so much.

What!?! Rob Starr was going to live at my house indefinitely. Amazing! Of course, about four seconds later I realized that this miracle might not really be amazing at all. I mean, wow, Rob Starr in my house for who knew how long was incredible but, holy shit, how was this going to go? Not only was I displaced from my room and all my stuff, but now I had to think about what I ate – like, all the time.

Anyway, that's how I found myself hanging out on Sunday night (*not* eating cheese popcorn), just me and Rob, in *our* TV room watching the game. I know what you're thinking; I probably wouldn't have been watching the game if Rob wasn't there and, okay, you have a point. But, I'm pretty sure that if you'd ever met him, you'd be there too, possibly even shouting 'Go Giants' at the top of your lungs.

The third miracle happened a week later but before I tell you about it, I must tell you a little bit about the crazy week leading up to it. I knew having Rob and Jake Starr in my house would be weird – and it was – but I had no idea how much it would affect things at school. As soon as the other kids found out that the Starrs were staying at my house, I was catapulted from virtual obscurity to something akin to a B-list celebrity. Tons of kids suddenly acted like they knew me – actual cool kids – popular juniors and seniors – were coming up to me in the lunchroom to ask about the Starrs. On Wednesday afternoon, two football players even stopped me in the hall to ask me how Rob was doing.

I tried my best to answer everyone's questions about Mrs. Gerber-Starr's health. I even started listening to all the medical stuff my parents discussed at the dinner table so I could answer people knowledgably. I graciously accepted all the get well wishes, promising to share them with Rob and the rest of the Starr family when I got home. And, although I took it all seriously – it was a serious matter after all – I must admit I was enjoying it a little. I liked being the one in the know – being the school's lifeline to their favorite son. I felt important for the first time, well…ever.

Unfortunately, the Starr's presence and my new-found fame came with a significant downside. I now had to pay a lot more attention to how I looked. I no longer had to deal with just the big things (like that crazy zit on my nose). Now I had to think about all sorts of little things like making sure my hair was clean (which it was most of the time anyway but maybe not *all* the time) and that the frizz around my forehead was smooth and that I'd plucked my eyebrows and that my mascara (which I was now wearing everyday) wasn't flaking. And, most importantly, that I wore cute clothes; a very big challenge for the likes of me.

You see, my everyday look consisted of jeans, a light blue, white or maybe striped button-down shirt, and the beat-up pair of moccasins I'd had since the end of seventh grade. I know – pathetic. But when no one is really looking at you, clothes just don't seem that important. When the Starrs moved in, however, the rock I'd been living under was shoved aside and the brutal rays of fashion were glaring down at my GAP boy's-department shirts and out-of-date shoes.

It was a pretty significant problem because it wasn't like there were piles of cute-girl clothes in my bureau that I'd forgotten about or anything. And sure, I thought about asking my mom, but I already knew she wouldn't understand. Unlike her friend, Madeline Gerber-Starr, my mother didn't care much about fashion. She would almost certainly say something like, 'what do you mean, honey? I just bought you two new pairs of jeans last month'. And even if she was willing to take me shopping, the clothes I needed and the clothes she'd agree to buy for me were as different as chocolate cake and brussels sprouts.

I settled for making sure my hair and makeup looked okay which meant I literally had to get up twenty minutes earlier. Who knew being visible was so much work? Not to mention that all the quality time spent with my blow dryer was sucking up critical study time – a pretty big deal considering I was in advanced placement everything. But that brings me back to the third miracle –Rob Starr was failing Trigonometry.

CHAPTER 3

WTF

October 19th continued

O kay so I probably shouldn't call Rob's poor performance in Trig a miracle. I'm sure failing anything must suck. I mean, if it had been me, I would have been freaking out. Not that he was. Or at least he didn't show it, which was impressive since we all knew that if he got less than a C in anything, he'd be kicked off the basketball team – Ellsworth High School law.

We probably wouldn't have even known he was failing except that one afternoon, when he was in our dining room trying to do his homework – which was a lot because he hadn't been to school in a week or more – he just kind of lost it and threw his math book across the room. My mom and I were in the kitchen and we both ran into the dining room to see what happened. He played it off like it was no big deal, but his cheeks and the tips of his ears were flushed with frustration.

My mom must have told my dad what happened because later that evening my dad brought it up. "Why doesn't Mia give you a hand with your Trig homework?" he suggested over dinner that night (spaghetti and meatballs by the way, which I love but couldn't eat because a) it's totally fattening, and b), I would end up getting it all over myself). I don't want you to think I was starving myself over a boy or anything because that's just stupid. I just planned my eating for when Rob wasn't around. And by the way, that meant that if I wanted breakfast, I had to get up even earlier than I already was.

"You know she's taking Trigonometry now, too," my father bragged, "since she managed to get through Geometry over the summer at math camp. And she's got a 97 average. Isn't that right Mia?"

I'm sure I must have looked like I was going to throw up because that's exactly how I felt. My father had just announced to the Starr family that I'd gone to math camp during the summer. That's right – while other girls were strolling the beaches of Belize in Brazilian bikinis, sipping mimosas or, okay, maybe just hanging by the club pool in cute tennis outfits sucking on strawberry smoothies – Mia Morgan was at math camp. MATH CAMP – was there ever a dorkier combination of words? I doubt it. He might as well have called me a "mathlete". To make matters worse, I said something completely math-campy in response like "Um, I'm not sure. I haven't gotten my score back on the last test." Jake had to slap his hand across his mouth not to laugh out loud.

Let's just pause here for a minute about Jake. Jake used to be okay. I mean he didn't always act like a douche. In elementary school we were even friends or at least friendly in the way you are with any kid you were in the kiddie pool with or raced to the Good Humor truck. And he was normal right through middle school, one of those kids who sort of hung out with everyone – some kids from my group, some sporty kids (he was a decent soccer player although not nearly as good at soccer as Rob was at basketball) and even with some of his totally dorky friends from elementary school. I even went with him to the eighth-grade dance (which had our mothers practically planning our wedding). But ever since we'd started high school, he'd become a total jerk. It took him all of ten seconds to jump on the wave of his brother's popularity and he'd been an asshole ever since. Not that I ever really saw him very much. We only had one class together – Art – and we certainly didn't sit together or anything. I'm not even sure why he was there. There were like three boys total in the class and it wasn't like they were friends of his. I guess he just thought it would be an easy grade.

I know you're probably wondering if he was as hot as Rob and the answer is; no. Don't get me wrong – he was cute, and plenty of girls thought so; I mean he was a Starr after all. He was tall and had the same sort of sandy-blondish-preppy-with-something-exotic-thrown-in look that Rob had, but Rob was taller, and his features were more perfect, his eyes were greener, and his lips were fuller and… Well, in other words Jake would have been considered pretty hot if Rob didn't exist. Now that I think of it, it must have kind of sucked for Jake to have the better version of himself around all the time.

Anyway, when my dad made the tutoring suggestion, Rob looked almost as uncomfortable as I did. What senior wouldn't be mortified by the idea of being tutored by a sophomore? Luckily, my mother had enough sense to change the subject and I escaped to the TV room as soon as dinner was over.

Before I go any further, I must state something that is imperative to my story and that is: Rob had a girlfriend – Chloe Olsen. They weren't officially dating at this exact point in time but that was only a matter of detail. Rob and Chloe had been together on and off since the seventh grade and everyone knew they were a couple even if they weren't currently "on".

Like Rob, Chloe was a senior and was the alpha girl in the most popular group of girls at Ellsworth. They called themselves the Baditudes – short for Bad Attitudes – a name they had selected in middle school. However, while the name made them sound sort of rebellious and anti-establishment, don't be fooled – they weren't – not even close. In fact, they were about as "basic" as you could be – you know, student government, prom committee, bake sales and, of course, cheerleading.

And just so you know, this name thing was big in Ellsworth. It was obnoxious for sure, but also sort of helpful. It gave us all a shorthand way to label each other. So, you might say something like "she's a Baditude but she dresses more like Heam Tottie" (a not-so-clever switch up of the words team and hottie in case you didn't get it) or "This is the Tostito's table" (which I believe was a reference to the "toasting" of marijuana *and* the subsequent consumption of corn chips) or "He used to hang out with the Frenchies (a name I assumed has something to do with kissing) but now he's dating an HB&P" (this name's meaning was an insider secret though most people thought it stood for Head Band and Pearls because this was clearly their style guide). Oh, and another thing. The guys didn't have groups. They were organized by their sport's teams (Basketballers, Lax Boys etc.) or by the girls they were dating as in "he hangs with the Frenchies since he started hooking up with…"

My friends and I totally goofed on the name thing. We spent hours trying to make up stupid-funny names for ourselves. At various times we called ourselves The Miss Understoods, The R2DCups, Drama Queens and W.T.F. which people thought stood for *What* The Fuck but if you were in our inner circle you'd know that it stood for *Why* The Fuck as in, Why the fuck would anyone give their group of friends a stupid name? Ironically, by junior year W.T.F. sort of stuck. Sometimes stuff just happens that way.

Anyway, Chloe Olsen, Rob's girlfriend, was a Baditude which, by definition, meant she was a cheerleader. And as cliché as it sounds, cheerleaders were a big deal at Ellsworth. You see, our cheerleaders were not only pretty and popular, they were also hard-core athletes who'd won States four times in the last eight years. People came to the games to watch them almost as much as they did to watch the basketball or football. Even if you couldn't care less about cheerleading, you sort of couldn't help but get into it. They were that good – their tumbling and dance moves and lifts, all done with military precision, synchronized down to the swing of their ponytails. And although I was as mesmerized as the next person, something about them always reminded me of dodgeballs; each one tough and bouncy, and even a little orange from too many spray tans.

Chloe was a flyer (of course) and perfect for the job. She was tiny but flawlessly formed, like a doll. My friends and I often made fun of her synthetic appearance – thick makeup and hair hardened with hairspray – but don't think for a minute she wasn't actually and honestly pretty. Strip it all away and she was the real deal, genuine article, couldn't-make-an-ugly-face-if-she-tried kind of pretty.

Rob and Chloe's relationship was part of all our lives in the same way that basketball was. Whether you wanted to or not, you were aware of how things were going – winning or losing – breaking up or getting back together. And just like with basketball, even if the season wasn't going well, the team was still a team. That's why, even though almost every girl in the school had a crush on Rob, few ever tried to get him, even during the breakups. Everyone knew he'd inevitably go back to Chloe, so, what was the point? You'd only end up alone in the bleachers, the rival of all.

But let's get back to the miracles. I had just settled into the couch to watch some bad teen TV when Rob came in and asked if

I'd mind watching the game. He was really nice about it – saying he could just watch it on his computer if I was really into whatever it was I was watching – as if there were some universe in which I might actually say "no" to Rob Starr. So, we ended up watching the game – or Rob watched the game and I watched him watch. At the first commercial break, Rob turned to me (luckily, I caught myself in time and had turned back towards the screen). He said, "So, what do you think?"

"Huh?" I replied wittily.

"About tutoring me in Trig?"

"Oh… sure."

"Tomorrow after school?"

"Sure."

And just like that I became Rob's tutor. Of course, I had to miss art club and band practice to do it but, hey, some things are just more important than personal growth.

CHAPTER 4

Trigonometry

October 20th

I spent almost an hour deciding what to wear to this math tutorial that was to take place in my very own dining room. Should I keep my school clothes on or change into some cute sweats and t-shirt? I opted for sweats, so I wouldn't look like I was trying too hard; though I fixed up my makeup a little and arranged my hair into a carefully constructed messy bun. My zit was all but gone; another small miracle in itself.

I'm not sure what you're thinking right now but let me assure you – I had no illusions. I wasn't clueless and I definitely wasn't confident enough to think that if I wore berry pink lip gloss or nice perfume, Rob Starr would suddenly see me as the girl of his dreams. Not at all. My goal in looking good was to appear acceptable, you know, not gross or weird. In other words, I just wanted Rob to think I was okay – nice, maybe – and not some total loser.

Besides, there was more to worry about than what I looked like. I was also concerned about the whole "tutoring" arrangement. Some of my friends were tutors (of course), and I'd heard the stories about how the jocks dumped on them – expecting them to write papers or do their homework for them – not even showing up to the sessions most of the time. I didn't know what I'd do if Rob assumed that was the situation.

But I needn't have been concerned. When Rob showed up, he actually seemed a little nervous. He made a couple of predictable pig-related cracks about our Trig teacher, Mr. Hansel, who was unfortunately round-faced and always a bit pink. Then he launched into the classic speech about how math is a huge waste of time because we're never going to use stuff like Trig in our real lives.

To be honest, I was not impressed with Rob at that moment. This particular argument about math always struck me as kind of lame – just a smart-ish sounding excuse for being lazy. Sure, math can be boring – so can Social Studies and Science and pretty much any subject in school. They all basically suck most of the time, but we all have to take them, and we all have to pass. And, I'm pretty sure they suck less if you're not failing them.

I didn't say any of this to Rob of course. I just listened to him until his nervous energy subsided enough for us to get going on the work. And after the first few minutes, it was clear – as I suspected – that he was *really* behind. He wasn't using the basic mnemonic SOH CAH TOA that we learned the first week and was even a bit shaky on some fundamental Geometry. I just acted like it was no big deal – everyone forgets stuff – and took him through it slowly. Eventually he started to catch on. After about forty-five minutes he pushed back his chair and smiled.

"You're really good at this," he said, running his hands through his shaggy, honey-colored hair. If Rob were a dog, he would be a golden retriever.

"Thanks. You're doing great."

He smiled again and then frowned. "I've got so much more though."

"I'm happy to keep going," I offered.

Rob laughed. "That's what she said."

"What?" I said, recognizing the joke a few seconds too late and probably turning bright red.

"Nothing, it's just something…anyway, I've gotta go. I have to go see my mom now." Rob's face grew serious.

"How is she?"

He sighed and ran his hands through his hair again and I forced myself to look at his face and not his flexing bicep. "She's asleep, you know, in a coma, so she doesn't even know we're there." On the last word, I heard a small catch of emotion in his voice. He cleared his throat. "Can we study again tomorrow? Oh, and my dad wants to know how much you charge."

"Oh, uh, tomorrow is fine and don't worry about the money. I'm happy to do it for free."

"That's what…"

"She said?" I finished for him.

He grinned. "Exactly."

Not surprisingly, my friends wanted to hear about Rob on the walk to school the next morning. Stephanie Xu, my best friend since middle school, (even though I kind of couldn't deal with her anymore), was waiting at the end of my front walk practically jumping up and down with anticipation. She was always like that – over-excited about everything. When we were kids, I thought she was the funniest person in the world but lately she'd been getting on my nerves. Don't get me wrong, she was a really good and loyal friend, and she had super cool fashion sense, but, like everything else, she took it too far. She was always completely over dressed for school. She wore bold colors and mixed patterns and while it would have looked amazing in a magazine, it looked a little crazy when everyone else wore mostly sweats or jeans. And she wore

bright red lipstick, like every day. On top of all that she talked and
laughed way too loud and well, now that we were in high school, it
was just kind of embarrassing sometimes.

That morning she kept insisting that *something* interesting must
have happened and I kept insisting that it hadn't. And that was the
truth of it. Sure, there were those jokes at the end that maybe someone might interpret as sort of flirty and the way Rob had grinned at
me had made me heart race. But telling Stephanie about that stuff
would have ruined it. Besides, what would be the point? Nothing
had happened or would ever happen between me and Rob Starr.

I saw Rob later that day at school. I was heading to gym class
with Jenna Perez, another sophomore, who happened to be quite
pretty in a sporty, glossy-haired way. He and his friends Justin
McCloud, a loud, showoff-y guy with a really good body but a little
too much acne, and Reynolds Prince, a totally gorgeous, totally
rich black kid who thought he was God's gift, were walking towards us. To my shock and delight, Rob nodded as we approached.
Justin, noticing Rob's attentions, turned as we walked by. 'Love me
some baby chicks,' he said, grabbing his crotch suggestively. It was
completely rude, and we probably should have said something, but
they were all so cute and popular, we just giggled stupidly, both of
us more flattered than offended.

When I got home my mother informed me that Rob was waiting for me in the dining room. Please understand that even writing
this down now, after everything, it still seems a little unreal. But
then, that Rob Starr should be waiting for me for any reason or
even be in my house was just one hundred percent weird.

Before I went in, I peeked at him through the doorway. He
looked tired – more than tired – exhausted. He was slumped forward over the table, leaning on his arm with his hand buried in
his hair. And for a moment, I understood just how bad he must be

feeling. He'd probably been up half the night worrying about his mom. Suddenly, I felt awful. I'd spent the last couple of weeks agonizing over how much I wasn't eating or what I should wear and in all that time I hadn't once genuinely considered what he was going through.

I grabbed some cookies and juice boxes from the kitchen. Yup, my mother still bought us juice boxes because 'they're just so easy,' which was totally at odds with her whole 'clean up the world' thing, but, hey, I guess some habits die hard – and brought them into the dining room. "Thanks," Rob said, his mouth almost instantly full of cookies. When I handed him a juice box he smiled and even with Oreos in his teeth it made me swoon. I know swoon is a cheesy word but there just isn't any other way to describe it – stomach turning upside down, shortness of breath, dizziness.

"God, I haven't had one of these in years," he said pulling the little straw off the juice box package.

Rob continued to look at me for maybe another two seconds and I felt my face get red, so I quickly sat down and opened my book.

We worked for about an hour and got through two days of homework. He could really focus when he wanted to. Even when his phone went off a couple of times, he didn't glance at it, which is more than I can say for myself. His phone was on the table between us, so I couldn't help but notice that the texts were from Chloe – a picture of her tiny tanned figure in a neon green bikini popping up on the screen each time the phone dinged. After the fourth time, he finally looked at it and swore.

"Is everything okay?" I asked realizing as soon as I said it that it was totally none of my business.

"Yeah, fine," Rob answered.

"We should probably stop for today."

"Yeah," he said sighing. "I have to go see my mom anyway."
Rob rubbed one eye thoughtfully. "My dad can't go, and he thinks
someone should be with her, even though she has no idea we're
there." He closed his eyes. "It totally sucks."

"Yeah," I agreed and then for some completely unknown reason added, "do you want me to come with you?"

Rob opened his eyes and looked at me.

"I mean if you don't want to go alone."

"Really?"

Just then, his phone went off again. And I swear I didn't mean
to look, but the phone was right there. On it was a picture of boobs.
They were Chloe's – not that I've ever seen Chloe's boobs before,
but you could just tell. 'To cheer you up!' the text read.

Rob grabbed the phone.

I must have turned about eight shades of red because Rob said.
"Sorry about that. She's an idiot."

"No, uh…I'm sorry, I shouldn't have… I didn't mean to…"

"It's okay. Besides, I swear she wants people to see. If she
didn't, she wouldn't do shit like that all the time." He sounded sincere and a little annoyed, but I couldn't really tell what he was
thinking. Was he just trying to be nice or did he really think Chloe
was an idiot for texting nudes of herself?

He stood up and stacked his books. "I gotta go."

I nodded. "Sure."

I sat there for a few moments contemplating the fact that I had
just seen Chloe Olsen's boobs. Was it only a couple of weeks ago
that I was watching old Disney shows in the afternoons? Now, I
was suddenly living in the same house with the most popular guy
in school and seeing pictures of his girlfriend's boobs – ex-girl-
friend's boobs – whatever.

And they were some seriously good boobs, on the big side, particularly for her size. I mean no wonder she wanted everyone to see them. My own boobs were smaller. Not so small that I got teased or anything – just not big – and one of them was noticeably smaller than the other. My doctor told me that was very common, but I was still self-conscious about it. I mean I certainly couldn't imagine feeling confident enough about them to want to text them to someone. It must be a good feeling to know someone wants to look at you that way.

Ellsworth High School Case #1141
Transcript of interview: March 21
Student: Mia Morgan
Counselor: Dr. Janis Dubrovski

Dr. Dubrovski: *So, you're saying you don't know if you were raped or not?*

Mia Morgan: *No. I mean... yes. I mean... I don't remember things clearly, but I'm pretty sure that specific thing didn't happen, and I think I would remember that so...no.*

Dr. Dubrovski: *So, it wasn't rape. Well, that's a relief, I suppose. But, in the pictures it does look...*

Mia Morgan: *I know what it looks like in the pictures but they're not real – I mean... it's not what happened.*

Dr. Dubrovski: *So, you are saying that the pictures are fake?*

Mia Morgan: *Not fake... faked. You know, edited and posed when I was...out of it. And they made it look... they made me look like I was...it looks really bad. Like I was into it. But I wasn't. It didn't happen like that.*

CHAPTER 5

Picture Day

October 21ˢᵗ

The next day was picture day. Not a big deal or anything but everyone did try to look at least marginally better than they normally do. I spent the better part of an hour straightening my wavy, frizzy, annoying hair and did my makeup better than just my usual mascara and lip gloss. When I came down to breakfast, I was surprised to find Rob was there wearing a jacket and tie.

"Morning," he said. "You look pretty."

I must have looked shocked because Rob chuckled. "What? You do. Your hair looks good like that."

"Thanks," I mumbled trying to regain my composure. "You do too." I said. Although in all honesty, he looked really tired again.

Rob nodded. "I have to wear a tie for the student government picture."

Did I mention Rob was senior class treasurer? The irony of this was not lost on his math tutor.

The rest of the morning was like walking around in a cloud because – in case you missed it– Rob Starr said I looked pretty. Okay, so I knew it wasn't a big deal or anything. I knew he was only being polite – just acknowledging I'd made an effort – but still, it wasn't like he'd said I looked *nice* – which is what most people would have said, or *cute* which would have been flattering but also might have meant that he still thought I was a little kid. Nope – he said *pretty* – which, in my opinion, is better than nice and cute put together.

What was even more amazing was that it sort of seemed like maybe Rob wasn't the only one who thought so. I swear that ever since Rob had moved in, boys at school had started to look at me differently. At first, I thought it was my imagination but no… guys were definitely giving me looks and not just looks but smiling and trying to make eye contact.

I could only conclude that my increased proximity to Rob (and the increased effort in my appearance) had somehow made me more attractive. Not surprisingly, I was clueless how to react to the attention – terrified I might do or say something stupid – like dropping the apple off my tray in the cafeteria when I was walking to my seat. Yup, that happened. It rolled under one of the Heam Tottie tables. I just kept walking and tried to pretend I didn't notice but…well…mortifying.

While all this was very new and actually kind of exciting (with the exception of the apple incident), my new status was seriously messing up my schedule. I had missed the last two band practices and the last two Art Club meetings. On top of that, Stephanie and Carmen Ruiz (another one of my good friends) got mad at me when I said I had to tutor Rob instead of joining their project group for Global History. The funny part was, they didn't really need me. Carmen was very likely going to be the valedictorian of our class, and Stephanie, while ditzy, was a solid A student. I suspected the real reason they were mad was that I – now officially – knew Rob Starr and was getting a lot of attention. I should have seen this as a warning sign – a foreshadowing of things to come – but I was too engrossed in my new experiences to give it a second thought.

So, before I go on, I need to explain something. In elementary school, I had tons of friends. Not that I was Miss Popularity or anything, but I never had to worry about not having friends. However something happened that summer between fifth and sixth grade. It was as if I'd missed some announcement that said it was time to stop playing with Barbies and Legos and to grow up and start liking boys. From the first day of middle school, I could tell something was wrong with me. Why was I the same goofy, Polly-Pocket-hoarding, friendship-bracelet-making kid, but everyone else had changed? The girls I used to hang out with almost every day after school suddenly had other plans. I was left out and hurt. I tried to make new friends, but no one seemed very interested. I lost my confidence and eventually I just gave stopped trying.

When I met Carmen and Stephanie the second week of seventh grade it was a huge relief for all of us. Turns out we had all gone through a brutally lonely and miserable first year of middle school. So, when we finally found each other, we swore to always be friends. We promised to never leave one another out or talk behind each other's backs. We vowed we'd be there for each other no matter what. And we swore that no new friend or boyfriend would ever come between us. At the time, it seemed like an easy promise to make – I'd finally found people who I could be myself around; kids I could trust. I never imagined that it would ever be hard to keep these promises or how quickly things could change.

I guess with all the recent events, I shouldn't have been surprised to find Chloe Olsen standing at my locker at the end of the day, but I was. I was very, very surprised. There she was in all her tiny glory wearing a cropped, pink #endbullying t-shirt, without a hint of irony. She was flanked by two other Baditudes. All three were looking at something on Chloe's phone and laughing.

Several feet away, trying to act casual, were Stephanie and Carmen who, although annoyed with me, were still apparently

willing to wait for me so we could walk home together. Or maybe
they just wanted to find out what Chloe Olsen had to say.

I waited several seconds for Chloe and the Baditudes to notice me,
but they either didn't or were pretending they didn't. Finally, I said,
"Uh, hi. Do you mind if I uh ...get in there?"

"That's what he said," said the taller of the backup-singer
Baditudes and they all cracked up. I should mention here that I,
like everyone else, had heard this joke a million times before. It
was really popular for a while in middle school and we used to
giggle about it back then knowing it had something to do with sex.
Of course, we'd probably said it at all the wrong times, not fully
understanding what we were suggesting. But now, when these girls
said it, it sounded like they really knew what they were talking
about. And when you're fifteen and kids – practically your own age
– are joking (knowingly) about sex it was pretty awkward for those
of us who were still in the dark.

Finally, Chloe looked up at my face and then slowly scanned
me up and down. When her gaze returned to my eyes she said, "Are
you Mia,"? pronouncing it My-ah when it should be Mee-ah, but
hell, who am I to correct Chloe Olsen?

"Yes..."

She frowned prettily. "So, Rob has been, like, staying at your
house, right?"

I nodded.

She smiled sweetly. "And you've been, like, helping him with
his Trig homework?"

I nodded again and cleared my throat nervously. But when I spoke
my voice was froggy. "I'm his tutor," I croaked, hoping she understood
that it was just a job – that I wasn't trying to flirt with him or anything.

"That's so nice of you," she said smiling generously. Her tone
reminded me of my kindergarten teacher, Miss Mruz.

"Oh...yeah... sure."

"You know we're all, like, counting on you My-ah. Rob *needs* to pass Trig."

"Yeah... definitely."

"And, well, I know I like, probably don't have to say this but... that's all he needs."

It didn't come out exactly like a threat. Her tone was sweet and sing-songy. But the general idea was clear. Stay away from Rob.

When they strolled away, Stephanie and Carmen came rushing up.

"Shhhhh," I hissed before either of them could speak. "Don't say anything until we're sure they're gone."

When the Baditudes were safely out of earshot, I conveyed the conversation to my friends. Stephanie was so excited, I thought she might faint. "Oh... my... God," she gasped hysterically, "Chloe Olsen thinks you're her competition!"

"No, she doesn't," I said – although Stephanie did kind of have a point. "She's just upset because Rob hasn't been answering her texts."

"What?" Carmen said. "How do you know that?"

"I don't. I mean, I don't know anything. Except that he's really stressed out about his mom and school and I think he's not acting like his normal self, is all."

"I don't blame him." Carmen said thoughtfully. "But really, what does he know about being normal anyway? He's like the most gorgeous person on earth!"

I did my best not to roll my eyes. Why did they always have to be so ridiculous? I headed home with the excuse that I needed to do a lot of homework, but the truth was, I just couldn't get away from them fast enough.

CHAPTER 6

An Unplanned Noise

October 21st Night – October 24th

W hen I got home, I ran into my mother and Rob rushing out of the house.

"It's Madeline..." my mother said breathlessly as they hurried toward the car.

"I'm coming with you," I said. Neither of them responded so I threw my backpack in the back seat and climbed in.

It was a long and awful night. 'Touch and go' was how the doctors described Mrs. Gerber-Starr. What the heck did that mean anyway? It certainly didn't sound very official – which somehow made it even scarier – like they didn't know what the hell was going on. Turns out they don't always know everything – doctors, that is. Up until this point, my only interaction with any of them was my yearly physical – and I still got stickers and a lollypop.

The lights in the hospital waiting room were too bright and the air was thick with the scent of synthetic lilacs coming from a plug-in room deodorizer near the door. The furniture was new-ish but heavy, framed in light colored wood with offensively cheerful blue and green cushions.

Rob paced the hall like a caged tiger. Jake sat several chairs away from the rest of us playing a game on his phone, which would have seemed kind of callus, except that every once in a while, I noticed him rub his eyes. He was pretending they itched or something, but I could tell he was crying a little. Rachel, still in her junior girl scout uniform, leaned against my mother, dozing.

I must have fallen asleep, too, because I woke up to the sound of the hospital gearing up for the day. A few minutes later, a doctor came out to inform us that Mrs. Gerber-Starr had finally stabilized. Two more doctors joined the first one and they spoke to my mother for several more minutes. I tried to listen, but their voices were hushed, and I was too tired to make much sense of it. Back then, at the beginning of the whole ordeal, I didn't understand any "hospital-speak" anyway. All I understood was that it was a huge relief. Every one of us cried a little, even Rob. After that, Mr. Starr stayed but the rest of us went back to the house – which is how we referred to our home now that we had permanent guests – and slept into the afternoon.

I woke up again, to the sound of someone tapping at my door.

"Come in?" I said.

Rob pushed the door open. He stood in the doorway in his pajama bottoms and no shirt. His skin was a light, sun-kissed color even though it was October. His shoulders and chest were neatly carved like the guys you see in underwear ads and there were long defined muscles down either side of his stomach where his hips and waist met.

"Hey," he said

"Hi."

"Can I come in?"

"Sure," I said sitting up more now – more than a little horrified that Rob was seeing me after a night of not having slept and then sleeping half the day. Sadly, that was the first thing I thought of.

Not, 'why is he in here?' or 'is something wrong?'. Nope, I thought 'oh no, I must look like shit'. And I'm sure I did since I'd been too tired to even wash my face. I had managed to pull off my jeans before getting into bed but was still wearing the shirt I had on the day before. My hair, well I didn't want to think about it, and I could feel the mascara caked in the corners of my eyes.

Rob walked into the room. He looked sleepy and by the way he smelled I could tell he hadn't showered. Not that he smelled bad or anything – just a little sweaty maybe and a bit like the hospital. I don't know why but it made me think about what people must have smelled like in Elizabethan times when they'd go the whole winter without ever taking a bath. I was just weird that way. I thought about really random stuff when I was nervous.

The guest room was kind of small. There weren't any chairs or anything. To be polite, I moved over and pushed the blankets aside, so Rob could sit on the bed. As soon as he got close to me, I could see that he'd been crying.

"Are you okay?"

He shook his head once and tears started streaming down his cheeks. "What if she dies?" he mumbled through a sob. Then he turned and looked at me "What if she *dies*?" he said again desperately. His nose was running now, and I handed him the tissue box from the bedside table. He took it gratefully. He cried a little while longer then blew his nose. I just sat there. I had no idea what to say.

"I'm really..." he said putting his head in his hands. He didn't finish, but instead started rocking back and forth a bit. At this point, I finally forgot about how I looked. I pulled myself out of the covers and crawled closer to him, laying my hand on his bare shoulder. His skin felt warm and smoother than I expected – not that different from my own. I don't know what I expected really – boy skin, I guess.

"It's okay," I said, hoping with all my heart that it was.

He nodded a little and leaned towards me, so my arm naturally moved around his shoulders. He lifted his head and turned, and I knew what was going to happen. I should have been shocked, but I wasn't. I knew Rob was going to kiss me and it was as if I'd always known – since the day of the accident when he'd first come into the house. Or maybe even before that – maybe even back when we were kids in the Starr's backyard – before we were old enough to even understand those feelings – maybe that's how it was with some people.

At first, his lips were dry and papery, and both our mouths were stale from sleep and I was worried for a moment that he would know I didn't know what I was doing. But then none of it mattered. Rob was kissing me as if he needed to, urgently, deliberately and I kissed him back somehow knowing how to even though I'd never really been kissed before. Oh, there had been a couple of times at Math Camp with this boy named Hector who kissed in a lazy way as if his tongue was too tired to move very much and once before that, at one of those parties where you pick someone's name out of a hat and then had to go kiss them in a closet. That time it was a kid named Brian and although he was my age, he hadn't gone through puberty yet, so I felt like I was kissing a fourth grader which, for the record, is really unappealing.

But just so we're clear, none of that was going through my mind this time. I was far too focused on what was happening, which was that Rob was kissing me or we were kissing each other, and it was amazing – like dancing or floating. And a part of me understood that this wasn't a typical first kiss. There was no hesitancy, no tentativeness like you see in the movies. This kiss – our kiss – was serious and insistent from the start and it grew with intensity until Rob suddenly pulled back and looked at me – his eyes were questioning, searching mine for something…permission maybe?

When I didn't move to stop him, he slipped his arm around my waist, pulling me towards him, half onto his lap and kissed the part of my neck where my throat and collarbone met. I moaned. Yup – actually made an unplanned noise. Then, I heard my name.

"Mia?" my mother called "Are you up? Do you want something to eat, honey?"

We jumped away from each other, my heart pounding in my ears. "I just woke up," I called back. "I'll be down in a minute."

"Okay, I'm making some eggs."

"Okay, great. Be down in a minute, Mom."

"Why don't you see if Rob and Jake are awake? Maybe they'd like some too."

"Yeah. Okay. Down in a minute."

At this point, Rob was standing. I couldn't look at him because he was clearly hard, which is difficult to hide in pajama pants. I didn't know where to look.

"I've got to get dressed," I said.

"Oh…" he said, "yeah, sure."

"Would you mind?" I indicated with my finger that I wanted him to turn around. When he did, I rushed to pull on some sweats and a clean shirt. Then I left him there standing at the foot of my bed.

I didn't see Rob again that day. I went to school to see if I could get my homework assignments from my teachers during their study hours. Rob went back to the hospital where his mom was "out of the woods" but still not awake.

I really didn't know what to think about the kiss. It was almost impossible to believe; it was like I'd dreamed it. But it *had* really happened and well, what the heck? Did he like me? Was that even possible? Or was it something else, like one of those things that just kinda happens and doesn't really mean anything at all? And now what? It wasn't like I was going to be Rob's girlfriend. That was too much to consider, too much to imagine even within the confines of my own head. Besides, Chloe was Rob's girlfriend – even though they weren't actually a couple at the moment. And holy shit if that was true – if Chloe was Rob's girlfriend – what did that make me?

With band practice and Rob's sports stuff and all the hospital visits, I didn't see Rob again until Friday – almost three full days later – in the school cafeteria. Normally we didn't have lunch during the same period, but there he was at "center court" – the name we called the table in the middle of the room – which was not officially but implicitly reserved for the Baditudes and the basketball team. Rob seemed totally normal, totally comfortable; laughing and flicking paper footballs through soda can goal posts. There was no sign of the desperate guy who'd shown up in my bedroom just a few days earlier. Chloe was there, too, but they were sitting several people away from one another and didn't appear to be "together". Maybe I was reading into it, but it seemed to me like she was trying to get his attention – talking and laughing too loudly – flirting with Mike Egan (the second cutest guy in school – or at least one of the top five if you're accounting for personal taste). At one point, she even sat on Mike's lap for a few seconds, but when Rob didn't react, she got up and started talking to a couple of her friends.

I literally couldn't take my eyes off their table. Stephanie and Carmen noticed, of course.

"What's up with you?" Stephanie asked annoyed that I hadn't been listening to the story of how she got her period in Mr. Tremont's class and how he wouldn't let her go to the girl's room until the end of the class (see, I was listening).

"You've been staring at center court this whole time," she added, as if I didn't know what she was talking about.

"I'm worried about Rob," I answered, which was kind of true, but not really. What I'd really been thinking was that Rob Starr – *the* Rob Starr – had come into my room and kissed me – seriously kissed me – and it didn't mean shit. Nothing had changed. I was still sitting at my lunch table with Carmen and Stephanie and Angelica – who was like my third best friend – and Jonah and Brandon – who were some of the goofy guys we hung out with – and Rob was still at his table with his friends. They didn't build bridges big enough to cross that kind of distance. But I couldn't say any of that.

"I know what you mean," said Carmen. "I saw Jake the other day and he seemed really out of it."

Carmen and Jake used to be friends in middle school – back when he used to hang out with us, before he decided to be a total douche.

"They say Mrs. Gerber-Starr is doing a little better," I said to change the subject, although not very much, I'll admit.

"That's good," said Carmen. None of us really knew what to say about that stuff. "We better go to English," she added.

We dumped our trays and were headed out of the cafeteria when someone grabbed me by the arm.

"Hey, Mia." Carmen, Stephanie, and I turned. It was Rob.

"Hey," he said again a little out of breath as if he'd been running to catch me. He nodded at Carmen and Stephanie.

"Hi," I managed, trying to contain my surprise. I glanced at Stephanie. Her mouth was hanging open.

"You guys go ahead," I said, giving her a slight push with my armload of books.

It took an uncomfortable few seconds for Stephanie to catch on and then she made a big thing of saying that they'd wait up for me outside of class. When they walked away Rob kind of laughed.

"So, can we study this afternoon? I just found out I have a Trig test on Monday."

"Oh, yeah sure," I said, even though I had already made plans to go get pizza after school with Carmen and Jenna and a couple of other kids.

"Great, see you at the house then."

As he headed back to his table, I saw Chloe Olsen looking at me. I quickly turned and left the lunchroom.

CHAPTER 7

The History of History

October 24th continued

I got home before Rob and ran upstairs to get ready. I put on some cute-ish, tight-ish sweatpants and a long sleeve t-shirt. Then I went to the bathroom and brushed my teeth. I figured even though Rob had already had an up-close experience with my worst breath, he didn't need to think I smelled that way all the time. While I was there, I figured I might as well wash my face and then reapplied a little blush and mascara and – what the hell – some lip gloss too.

I waited for him in the kitchen, debating whether to have something to eat. I decided no, because a) he could walk in anytime and b) I had just brushed my teeth. However, when Rob didn't show up for another forty-five minutes, I regretted it. When he did finally get home, it wasn't like I could say anything about him being late. I mean we hadn't said four o'clock. I just figured he meant four o'clock because that was the time we'd met before… but we never said an exact time.

"So… ready?" Rob asked helping himself to an apple. I nodded and headed into the dining room. He followed me and let the door swing shut behind him.

We worked on Trig for about the time it took Rob to eat his apple which was three minutes, tops. Then he got up to throw away the core.

"Listen," he said as he came back into the room, "I hope you don't mind but I just can't really concentrate right now, you know?"

The truth was I didn't mind at all. I guess I probably should have. I mean, I'd blown off my friends to help him study for his test. And, he was late – kind of. But none of that really mattered. In fact, I was relieved. The whole thing was so awkward. Was I supposed to pretend nothing happened? That we'd never kissed? It was better that I just get out of there – just head up to the guest room (which I'm just going to call my room from now on for simplicity's sake) and hang out by myself until dinner.

"No problem," I said nodding and hoping my tone sounded understanding. I stood up and started to get my papers together.

But then Rob sighed. He looked up at me with a sad, closed mouth smile. "Don't go," he said. His voice was thick. He cleared his throat.

I stopped what I was doing- which wasn't anything but nervously moving papers around -and sat back down. "Are you okay?" I asked. Sometimes I couldn't believe how selfish I could be. Here I was obsessing over how uncomfortable I felt about me and Rob, and had yet again, forgotten the part where Rob was dealing with the fact that his mother might be dying in the hospital.

He nodded, then shook his head. "I'm sort of okay when I'm at school. You know, it's like… distracting. But as soon as I'm alone I get really freaked." He paused and looked into my eyes. "And even when I'm with all my friends, I'm constantly pushing my thoughts out of my head, you know? Just acting like everything's okay even though it's not."

We had shifted in our chairs and were facing each other now, each with one arm on the table – our hands only inches apart. Slowly, Rob moved his hand across the small distance and put the tip of his first finger on my pinky and my whole body felt like I'd been lit on fire. Then, with his eyes focused on where our fingers were touching, he said, "but when I'm with you I feel… I don't know…steadier."

"Steadier?"

"That didn't come out right," he said quickly, his eyes still fixed on our hands. "I mean, it's true, but it sounds boring which it totally wasn't or… isn't."

I could feel the blood in my cheeks. I wanted to pull my hand away and grab onto the edge of the table, but I couldn't move.

"You aren't mad about the other day, are you?" Rob asked looking up, his eyes searching my face, his words coming out in a rush. "I mean I hope you're not. But you sort of ran out of the room and I realized that you might think I was trying to get over on you – you know, like…take advantage of you or something … and you've been so nice and your family has been so nice and I don't know… it was kind of weird with everything else going on. I mean I don't know if you even like me that way."

By this point, I couldn't really process what I was hearing. He was talking about the kiss of course but at first it sounded like he was trying to tell me that it was too weird, and he was sorry he did it, but then it also sort of sounded like maybe he meant something else.

"You're right," I gambled.

"I am?"

"Yeah, it was a little weird."

"Right," he said pulling his finger away and nodding. "I'm sorry."

Was I crazy or did he actually look disappointed? He stood up and started to put his books in his backpack. I followed his lead and finished collecting my things. We stood there, packing up in silence for a minute and for some reason, I felt like I might cry. I was completely confused about what was happening. Had I just dissed Rob Starr?

I took a deep breath. "You don't have to be sorry about kissing me if that's what you mean. I'm not… mad or anything. It was okay... you know… it was nice."

Rob stopped and turned to me. "It was?" he said hopefully, his head tipped to one side. He looked so innocent and sincere I couldn't help but smile.

"Yeah," I said, quietly.

"*Really* nice?" He asked. One eyebrow was up and there was a smile pushing at the corners of his mouth.

"I guess..." I said looking down at the papers – not that I could actually see anything, "really nice."

"Ha!" he grinned. "I don't know who you've been kissing, Mia Morgan, but that kiss was not *nice*."

For a moment, my heart stopped. Was he goofing on me? Was this some kind of cruel upperclassman thing – the old get-the-nerdy-sophomore-to-admit-she-liked-kissing-you-then-completely-humiliate-her joke?

But then Rob stepped closer to me. He put his arm around my waist and pulled me towards him, so our bodies were touching. Then he put his mouth to my ear and whispered.

"That was the hottest kiss in the history of history."

And then we were at it again. His mouth, this time, was sweet like apples and for a few minutes I was lost in the feel of him but then we shifted a little and something – his notebook maybe – fell off the table with a loud thump and I was suddenly acutely aware

that we were in my dining room – I could hear the kitchen clock
ticking and the sound of the refrigerator – and I realized that anyone could walk in at any minute.

I pulled back. "We have to stop. We can't be like this in my
house," I said.

His eyes were wet and shining and his breath was short. He
nodded. "Meet me at the bonfire tomorrow night."

"Huh? No. I... uh... I'm not sure that's such a good idea," I
said.

"Why not?"

"I don't know...you know...I don't really know your friends
and..."

"Don't worry about my friends," he said cutting me off. "If
you're with me, they'll be fine."

"I don't think..." I began again but Rob pulled me closer to
him.

"Please Mia? I need you near me."

Now, how do you argue with that?

CHAPTER 8

ORD

October 24ᵗʰ & 25ᵗʰ

So now you know how all this stuff between Rob and me began, and at this point, I could just fast forward to the night of the bonfire. I could skip over the twenty-five or so hours in between because I'm sure (or at least I hope) you want to know what happens next. And that is certainly how it works in most books. Months go by with the turn of a page. In the movies, weeks of waiting, or practicing or studying is always set to some pumped up soundtrack – as if all the difficult stuff in life can be accomplished in the course of a short music video. Well, I'm here to tell you that waiting for something – especially something you really hope will happen but are not sure will actually happen – is un-fun no matter what song is playing.

So, it's no big surprise that the twenty-five hours between the time Rob mentioned the bonfire and the actual event just totally sucked. Not that anything terrible or tragic happened. In fact, very little happened at all except for the all the craziness happening inside my head. You see, I had a serious case of something my friends and I jokingly called ORD or Obsessive

Repulsive Disorder (a somewhat insensitive twist on Obsessive
Compulsive Disorder which is, of course, a very real and con-
cerning condition).

So, what is ORD exactly? It is the act of obsessively focusing
on a someone who you are romantically interested in, who has *not*
definitively demonstrated similar interest in you.

Telltale signs of ORD include one or more of the following;
1) the inability to think or talk about anything else besides the ob-
ject of your obsession – often to the point of driving your friends
insane, (hence the "Repulsive" part), 2) assigning deeper meaning
to your obsession's words and/or actions, 3) social and sometimes
physical stalking of your obsession, and perhaps worst of all, 4)
exaggerating and/or lying about interactions you may (or may not)
have had with said person.

Personally, I was always kind of smug about ORD. I was
certain I would never allow myself to get that crazy over a boy.
Besides, I had too much going on with school and band and art
club to get caught up in something that was clearly a waste of time.
I mean when you think about all the girls in all the high schools
in all the world – the combined millions of hours that could have
been spent on other things – actual important things – change-the-
world, make-it-a-better-place kind of things (maybe even find a
cure for ORD); it's just depressing. But for some unknown reason (insecurity? biology? the media?) so many of us end up here,
acting in ways we never imagined we would and, as in my case,
despite my smugness and basic common sense.

My ORD began almost immediately after leaving Rob
that afternoon. I went up to my room and sat on the bed. My
heart was thudding, and my stomach clenched. I wanted to call
Stephanie, but I didn't know what I would say. I couldn't just
tell her that Rob had asked me to the bonfire seemingly out of

nowhere. I'd have to explain everything from the beginning. She didn't know about the night we spent at the hospital and I hadn't told her about the kissing. She'd probably feel betrayed that I hadn't said something right away. But it was Rob Starr we were talking about here – THE Rob Starr- and it was very likely she'd get overly excited and start shrieking and OMG-ing, or worse, post something about it, which would be a complete and a total nightmare.

Of course, there was also the possibility that I was avoiding telling Stephanie because – once she got through her embarrass- ingly childish reaction, she'd probably tell me I was bananas to even think of going to the bonfire with Rob Starr considering how mad it would make Chloe Olsen and well, then she'd have a real point. And, Chloe was just one of the many serious considerations I was dealing with.

Such as:

1) Chloe Olsen (as previously noted but worth repeating)
2) Chloe Olsen's friends (scary)
3) Rob's friends (also scary but in a different way) I mean, just the thought of Rob and his friends casually running into me and all my friends made me hyperventilate. I know how aw- ful that sounds – my friends were super nice people – but they were also mostly demi-geeks like me, and some were actual full-on nerds. The boys were particularly bad – not even on the same planet as Rob and the other jocks. None of them were re- motely athletic and most were still in that super awkward stage where their voices cracked when they spoke. They were all pimples and Adam's apples and narrow, marching-band shoul- ders that curved inward like question marks, punctuating the

yet unanswered question of sexual orientation. The girls were only marginally better; loud and ridiculous – as previously described – but at least some of them were on their way to being reasonably attractive. Not that it mattered. There was nothing cool about any of them.

4) My lack of cute-girl clothing (more on this later)
5) And, this is a biggie, logistics; by which I mean I had none – like where and when Rob thought we were going to meet up because we certainly couldn't go together – as in a date – because, oh my God, can you imagine if my parents thought Rob and I were dating and living in their house, together, at the same time? Which is clearly reason number 6.

And if you're wondering…no, I couldn't ask Rob for any of the logistics because – well…honestly, I don't know exactly why not – just that I couldn't. I guess I imagined that if I did, it would seem like I didn't know where to go or what to do (which I didn't). And I was convinced that if I were older or cooler or both, I would.

By the following afternoon I still hadn't seen or heard anything from Rob. With only hours to go before the bonfire, I decided that my best bet was to assume Rob either forgot (humiliating) or changed his mind (humiliating to the tenth power).

I tried to convince myself to get over it. He probably regretted asking me like four seconds after he left the dining room. He'd probably only kissed me because he was sad about his mother or worse. Maybe, since he and Chloe had broken up, he was just horny and looking to get over on someone. So, it was probably better in the long run that he hadn't texted me or anything because, really, there was no chance of someone like him ever actually being into someone like me.

And while I knew that all these thoughts were logical and that I was probably right about what Rob was thinking (or, more accurately, *not* thinking), there was still a tiny part of me – like maybe three-percent – that refused to fully accept it – refused to believe that I'd really gotten it all so wrong. And that three-percent voice kept asking questions like; if he didn't like me, why had he invited me to the bonfire in the first place? And why did he tell me he felt *steadier* when I was around? Who would say something like that and not mean it?

So, after hours of overthinking, I concluded that my only choice was to go to the bonfire with my friends and not tell them anything about Rob. And if he saw me, and let's say he nodded or said hi to me or something (because he is, in fact, living in my house and it would be totally rude if he didn't), I would very casually nod back or said hi (because that's how you act when you've hooked up with someone but it was just totally casual), and no one would be the wiser. In other words, if Rob did decide to blow me off, I'd be the only one who'd know it. And if on the tiniest chance that he did want to hang out with me, well I would figure that out if it happened.

And if you're wondering if I knew this was a bad plan at the time, the answer to that is yes. Yes, I did.

CHAPTER 9

The Vanity of the Bonfire

October 25th continued

S o, that was my final decision: I was going to the bonfire and I was going to be totally chill about it, which left only one major thing – the matter of what to wear.

This was a new and difficult challenge for me. Normal Me wouldn't have given it much thought – jeans, a hoodie and maybe a down vest. I mean it was going to be mostly dark out – right?

But now I had to deal with the very real possibility that I might see Rob (and all his friends) – even if it was only to walk by him and nod – and suddenly it seemed like the most important thing on earth that I *didn't* look like Normal Me.

I could tell you it's because I wanted Rob to think I was pretty or because I didn't want the Baditudes to think I was totally pathetic, but there was more to it than that. You see, ever since Rob kissed me, something inside me had sort of switched on. I felt more real, more important, more like I mattered somehow. And it made me wonder. Had I missed something? Maybe (a very small but persistent maybe) I wasn't as tap-water ordinary as I thought.

Don't get me wrong, Most of the time, I still felt like that insecure, dejected girl from middle school. I certainly didn't think I was suddenly popular or beautiful or that all the guys at school were in love with me. But deep inside me, and perhaps somewhere deep inside all of us, is the hope that there is more to us than meets the eye. Isn't that why we all love the story of Cinderella or King Arthur or Harry Potter – that moment of discovery when the main character realizes that they are somehow better and more special than they ever imagined?

And in my case, it wasn't a fairy tale – it had happened – sort of. Rob Starr was my letter from Hogwarts, my sword in the stone, my real-life Prince Charming. I guess what I'm saying is, I was tired of being the old me. I was ready to transform.

Luckily, I had Stephanie. Yup, believe it or not, despite her juvenile, often obnoxious personality, Stephanie had really good clothes. Her mom was some famous fashion blogger or something which meant that Stephanie was that kid who had the cool brands before anyone else had ever heard of them.

However, since I'd used up most of the afternoon waiting around at home hoping to run into Rob – by the time I was heading out to Stephanie's it was pretty late. I grabbed my jacket and ran into the kitchen to tell my mother I was leaving. She was sitting at the table staring into an empty coffee mug. She was crying.

"What's wrong?" I asked. Of course, I should have known what was wrong. One of her good friends was in a coma and she was worried – duh. She straightened up and wiped her eyes. They were red and tired-looking.

"I'm fine. I'm just worried about Madeline."

"Oh…did something happen?" I asked, not sitting down.

My mother shook her head. "Nothing new. No…change." She blew her nose into a tragically overused tissue. "Where are you going?" She said, noticing my jacket.

"The bonfire's tonight."

"Oh, right, Jake mentioned it to me. Are you going with him?" She sounded hopeful. "He's been having a bit of a rough time."

I cringed. Did she really expect me to ask Jake Starr if he wanted to go with me to the bonfire? My mother was famous for this kind of why-don't-you-all-go-together stuff.

"Uh…I've already got plans to go with Steph."

"Well… couldn't the three of you go?"

So, at this point – if I'm sticking with my honesty thing – I've got to admit that the entire time I was talking to her – I just wanted to be out of there. It was going to take me a while to figure out what to wear and I wanted to get to the bonfire while it was still light enough to look around for Rob. But my mother just kept talking about Jake, saying that he's having a hard time, getting into some trouble at school – something about a broken windshield… swears it wasn't him. And then there was the money missing from her wallet…

Wait—what? "Are you saying Jake stole money from you?" I said. Wow, what a jerk.

"Honestly, honey, I don't know. He says he didn't take it. But I'm sure I had sixty dollars in my wallet this morning." She shook her head.

"Yeah…well, that settles it. Besides, even if I wanted him to come with us, I doubt he would. He thinks I'm a geek."

"Oh, I don't think…"

At that moment Jake walked into the kitchen. He looked kind of rumpled, as if he'd been asleep.

"Hey," he said to me with an uninterested lift of his chin.

"Hi and uh… bye," I said, taking advantage of the interruption. "See you later probably," I added for my mother's benefit. Then I was out the door and running down the street to Stephanie's.

Please understand, I knew I was being selfish. But I just wasn't thinking straight. All I could focus on was the fact that I was going to (or probably going to) see Rob and that I had to get myself ready. And it seemed like the most important thing in the world at the time.

Stephanie was awesome that night. Delighted by my sudden interest in clothes, she indulged me with her expertise, no questions asked. She straightened my hair and did my makeup for me. She even let me borrow some super expensive riding boots and a beautiful, blue cashmere sweater that fit perfectly.

I felt glamorous walking down the street in her gorgeous boots with my pin-straight blow out whipping around me in the October wind. She was a great friend despite her ridiculousness. I should have been more grateful, but I was so caught up in my own movie I don't even remember thanking her.

Ellsworth High School Case #1141
Transcript of interview: March 21
Student: Mia Morgan
Counselor: Dr. Janis Dubrovski

Dr. Dubrovski: *Okay, well, I am hoping you can tell us exactly what did happen. For starters, it appears that there are two boys in the photographs with you. Is that correct? (pause) Please try and remember to answer aloud, Mia. The sound equipment can't capture you nodding your head.*
Mia Morgan: *Oh, yeah, sure...sorry.*
Dr. Dubrovski: *So, two?*
Mia Morgan: *Yes*
Dr. Dubrovski: *And who else?*
Mia Morgan: *Huh?*
Dr. Dubrovski: *Who else was there? Obviously, someone was taking the pictures. Was it another boy?*
Mia Morgan: *Uh...no.*
Dr. Dubrovski: *So it was a girl?*
Mia Morgan: *Yes.*
Dr. Dubrovski: *And do you know them?*
Mia Morgan: *Who?*
Dr. Dubrovski: *The kids that were there with you that night?*
Mia Morgan: *Um, kind of. Not really.*
Dr. Dubrovski: *What do you mean, kind of?*
Mia Morgan: *I...everyone kind of knows them. They're...*
Dr. Dubrovski: *Popular?*
Mia Morgan: *I guess.*

CHAPTER 10

The Bonfire

October 25ᵗʰ Night

The evening was gorgeous – crisp and cool and the sun was taking its time to set, casting everything in a coppery-gold. The moment we arrived at the soccer field we ran into Carmen and Jonah and a few minutes later Brandon and Eric showed up in their marching band uniforms. Everyone told me how good I looked, and some of the boys even acted a little goofy around me as if they were meeting me for the first time – as if most of us hadn't been in the same class every single year since elementary school. And I must admit – though I had absolutely no interest in any of them – there was something sort of fun about the whole thing. Maybe I was just nervous, but I caught myself flipping my hair a lot and laughing a bit louder than I normally do. After a half hour or so, our group had grown to nine or ten and we wandered around, like everyone else, from the food tables to the raffle tents to the carnival games and back. As it grew darker, the air grew colder and people started to move towards the center of the field. They positioned themselves around the bonfire which, at this point in the evening, was just a huge pile of wood stacked in a teepee shape with a stuffed scarecrow in the rival team's football jersey propped up on top. Most of the football team was already there and all of the cheerleaders. A couple of the cheer girls practiced their moves – a series of short jerky movements punctuated with an occasional standing back handspring (yeah, they were that good). Others were mulling around with large letterman jackets hanging from their shoulders; the green, satiny fabric was metallic and bug-like in the dimming light.

Just around sunset, Coach Pearson blew the whistle and the band started playing. If you're wondering why me and my flute were not involved, it was because I played in the jazz band, not the marching band. And thank God, because I would have died of embarrassment if I had to wear one of those uniforms in front of Rob. Everyone gathered around the bonfire as the cheerleaders did some fairly amazing stunts and shouted those perennial favorites "S-U-C-C-E-S-S" and "We're Gonna Win Tonight" and of course "Gimme an "E" (continue spelling Eagles here). While they cheered, my friends and I made snide remarks about them – how conformist and sexist cheerleading was – even the boys made cracks, though they could barely keep their eyes in their heads when Chloe and her cohorts bounced by.

Finally, as the sun went down, Coach Pearson lit a torch-thingy and stepped over the low circle of rope to light the fire. We all stood together in a dense circle, teachers, kids, parents, and watched as the flames climbed up the pyre. Just as they reached the scarecrow at the top, I felt someone behind me.

"Been lookin' for you," Rob said into my hair. I caught the skunky smell of beer on his breath. Not that I cared – not that it even registered really. He slipped his arms around my waist and I was suddenly paralyzed. My heart pounded in my temples. I hadn't made the whole thing up; Rob Starr was there – his arms around me.

Rob pulled me closer and set his chin on the top of my head. And for the briefest moment, I forgot about everything else. I let myself lean back into him and closed my eyes – the sounds around me softened by the fabric of his jacket.

We stood that way for a maybe ten seconds, with the blaze of the fire warming the front of me and Rob warming the back. It was hold-your-breath perfect, like the moment the sun touches the ocean at the end of a long beach day or right before a thunderstorm cracks open, when the air is filled with the soft thrill of electricity, and you make it to shelter in the nick of time. But when I opened my eyes, I saw Jake. He was staring at us from the other side of the fire, his mouth hanging open in stunned surprise.

Reality came rushing back like the jump to light speed. I was suddenly acutely aware of everything and everyone. I tensed up, pulled away from Rob's embrace and turned around.

"Hi, You," he said smiling and I could tell he was buzzed. Not that I'd had a lot of experience with those things but enough to know what it looked like.

"Hi," I said looking around nervously.

"Rock Sta, Sta, Sta, Staaaar!" Justin boomed as he barreled up to us and attempted to chest-bump Rob, literally knocking me out of the way. He was drunk.

"Where is everyone?" he asked Rob.

Rob tipped his head towards the fire and the football team and the cheerleaders.

"I mean everyone else," Justin snorted.

"Out by the bleachers," Rob said.

"Soo, whadda ya doing here?"

Rob smiled and glanced at me. Remarkably, Justin put two and two together. "Ah…some fresh meat, huh?" he commented as if I didn't have ears. "Tempting…" he said looking me up and down, but I told Mike and Reynolds we'd meet up with them. I've got the goods." He patted his jean jacket pocket for emphasis. I figured this meant weed but I was even less familiar with that than I was with alcohol.

"Cool," Rob said grinning. "How much do I owe you?"

Rob reached into his pocket and pulled out three twenties. Sixty dollars. A half a thought – my mom's missing money – flickered through my mind. But there was just no way it could have been Rob.

"Later, dude – not here," said Justin, as if he were some kind of expert on how these deals went down.

Rob tucked the money back into his jeans and draped his arm around my neck. The three of us started walking towards Porter's – the adjacent field where the football games were played. We had already gone several yards when I remembered my friends. I knew I couldn't invite them along, but I had to say something – tell them where I was going at least. But when I turned, I saw we were already too far away for me to say anything at all.

They seemed small, all huddled together, not far from where Rob and I had been standing. Every one of them was watching me with the same disapproving expression – as though I'd done something terrible – as if there were a dead body lying on the ground between us. I tried to make eye contact with Stephanie, but we were already too far away. I shrugged. She had to understand.

It was a long walk to the other field and much colder than it had been near the fire. Rob's arm was uncomfortable around my neck, but I didn't try to adjust it for fear he might suddenly realize it shouldn't be there in the first place. I'm sure my nose was red, and I could feel it starting to run; and before I considered what I was doing, I wiped it on the sleeve of Stephanie's sweater. Hey, what else could I do?

As we got closer to Porter's field I figured out where we were going. At the far end, past the bleachers, was a huge water pipe, tall enough for even a tall guy to stand in if he positioned himself right in the center. It connected the field to a muddy creek that ran along the highway, probably there in case of a flash flood. I'd never understood the attraction of "the tunnel"– it was cold and damp and there was always a trickle of water running down the middle of the "floor" even when it hadn't rained in weeks – but I knew it was where a lot of kids went to get high. Don't ask me where I got that information. I just knew it. Everybody did.

Inside the tunnel was even colder and much darker than it was outside. The only light came and went as cars on the highway sped by. There were probably ten kids there already, mostly Rob's friends. I recognized the shapes of Mike Egan and Steve Pitman who were both teammates of Rob's.

A note on Mike Egan: I sort of liked him – I mean before Rob – and not actually *liked* him but kind of crushed on him. Of course, I crushed on Rob, too, because you couldn't help it, but Rob was just too far out of reach to really consider. Mike was in my Spanish class so I saw him almost every day. He was handsome but short – just a couple of inches taller than me – and he had some pimples – which by high school rules made him more *possible* than Rob. I also kind of liked him because he was the first boy who had ever paid attention to me. It's embarrassing to admit, but the first few times he talked to me, I actually thought he liked me. It took me at least four weeks of classes to realize he acted the same way with everyone.

Anyway, he was there, talking to some Frenchie, who were always instantly recognizable by the hard, dark line of makeup they liked to wear around their eyes. There was also a couple macking down by the far end. But most of the kids were just standing around

Reynolds, who was tapping a keg and trying to convince some other kid – a sophomore I recognized from the basketball team – to go back to the bonfire and snag some cups from the food tents.

All the guys were pumped to see Justin and Rob and got particularly loud when Justin produced a pipe and baggie from his pocket. Beers were poured into the few available cups and Rob handed his to me. "We'll share," he announced, not that anyone cared or even acknowledged I was there. Now you may be thinking – how rude – or that I should have been insulted or something – but really, who are we kidding? I was lucky to be there, and I knew it. I was mostly just concentrating on not doing something embarrassing.

I took a sip of the beer. It was warm-ish and a little flat and I couldn't really say I liked it. Not that it was the first time I'd tasted alcohol or anything. My parents let us have some wine on Christmas Eve and my dad gave me a taste of some disgusting brown beer on St. Patrick's Day, but this was the first time I'd drank anything outside of my own house. I took another sip, a big one.

"You gonna share that or what?" Rob said kiddingly. I handed him the cup and he swallowed what was left in it in one large gulp. Then he left me to fill it up and I felt instantly exposed. Someone had lit the weed pipe and a cloud of heavy, skunky smoke filled the small space.

"Well, hello there," said Reynolds sliding his arm around my shoulder as he blew out a long stream of smoke. "Welcome to The Tunnel of Sins." He smiled dangerously. His smooth, dark skin looked shiny in the headlights. He had the pot pipe in his hand, and he held it out to me. "Ever done this before?" he asked.

I shook my head.

"Not to worry," he said handing me the pipe and turning closer to light it. "It's really simple. Just inhale it directly. It's not like a cigarette, you don't take the smoke in your mouth first."

I nodded. That probably would have been helpful if I'd ever smoked a cigarette, which I hadn't.

"It burns a bit though so be ready," he added as he flicked the lighter to life.

"That's what she said," someone said.

Rob laughed, now back at my side with a full beer. "Why would she say that, dude? Have you got VD or something?"

"Now boys, VD is no laughing matter," said Justin doing a fair imitation of Mr. Grant the Health teacher.

"You should know Justin." This from one of the Frenchies.

"Yeah, and we all know where I got if from, Trisha."

Everyone laughed, including Trisha.

While this was going on, Rob had slipped his arm around my waist and nuzzled his mouth to my ear so no one else could hear him, "You don't have to do this if you don't want to," he whispered. Okay, kind of sweet, right? And just when you were thinking that maybe he was a jerk.

I took a deep breath and looked around and I realized Rob was right. No one seemed to care about whether I was going to smoke or not. In fact, they weren't paying attention to me at all. They were just doing whatever they were doing – joking around, making out, drinking beer. It was nothing like those cheesy teen movies about peer pressure where the "bad kids" are taunting some poor soul into doing something wrong. And it struck me how so many of the books and TV shows and especially parents got it so wrong. Their little Jasmin or Simon or Chris would never smoke pot – and if they did, it was only because the bad kids *made* them do it. But at that moment I realized that wasn't really what happens at all. The truth was, I wanted to smoke, because I wanted to know what it was like. And yes, because it felt great to be included. And because it was kind of exciting to be doing something that might be a dangerous or that might get me in trouble. And the kids I was with were hardly the "bad kids". These kids were good students and star athletes. Hell, I was with Rock Starr basketball boy – not exactly the menacing social deviant parents fear. Yet here he was drinking and smoking pot which, apparently, he did quite often.

So even though I hadn't planned on smoking pot that night and maybe not ever, I couldn't really think of a reason why not. I certainly didn't want to make a big deal out of *not* doing it. It would only make everyone uncomfortable and embarrass Rob.

I took the pipe and put it to my mouth. The mouthpiece was like an oval wooden bead. The opening at the end was a little wet with other people's saliva which was kind of gross.

"Slowly," Reynolds warned.

I inhaled; maybe a bit too hard because I got some of the pot in my mouth along with the smoke. It tasted ashy and bitter. I resisted the urge to spit it out.

"Good job," said Reynolds, "Now hold the smoke in for a couple of seconds and blow it out." I did what he said but when I exhaled, barely anything came out. To tell the truth, I was sort of relieved. Maybe I didn't do it right. Maybe I wouldn't feel anything.

Rob took the pipe from me and took a big hit off it, making a big deal of how much he'd inhaled – barking back his cough – as if he could barely hold it in. Then he let out an enormous cloud of smoke and a couple of people cheered.

The pipe went around again and after a few minutes, things changed. The lights from the highway were round and cast a cyclone of shadows inside the tunnel. The sounds had a blanketed quality like they do on snowy mornings. Someone said something, and everyone laughed as if it were the funniest thing in the world – even me – although now I can't remember what it was, and honestly, I'm not sure I even heard it back then.

After a few more sips of beer Rob started kissing my neck. He led me down to the far end of the tunnel and leaned me back against the curved wall. It was nice – kissing Rob's warm, beer-sweetened mouth in the cold October air – but I wasn't as into it as I had been before. He was drunk, and his kisses were sort of sloppy. Plus, I had the odd sensation that I was there but not there. I was both kissing Rob and watching myself kiss him. Which was probably why I heard them coming before anyone else did – or maybe I'd been waiting for them – anticipating the moment without realizing it. And then, there it was – Chloe's false, loud laugh in the distance. Rob was oblivious. I had to practically push him away from me.

"What?" he complained.

"Chloe." I said.

"Fuck." Rob shoved his fingers into his hair, "Listen, don't let her get to you, okay?" He paused, thinking. "We'll just go. I have to get you home anyway."

Okay, so I can't say I was happy about Rob's reaction. Was he surprised Chloe was there? I mean, where else would she be? Once the cheering part of the bonfire was over, it seemed obvious she'd go wherever her friends hung out. But maybe this wasn't obvious to Rob or maybe he was just used to having things go the way he wanted them to. Anyway, about two minutes later the tunnel was filled with kids; mostly football players and cheerleaders. Since Rob and I were at the far end, there was no other way to get out but through the crowd. Rob took hold of my hand.

As I followed him through the crush of bodies, I understood a little of what it might be like to be famous or more accurately, what it would be like to date someone famous. Everyone turned towards him as he passed, some even reached out to touch him, eagerly waiting for him to notice them. And Rob complied with an easy confidence – graciously sharing his attention among his admirers.

He pulled me along behind him as if it were the most normal thing in the world – certain that any decision he made would be acceptable to his fans – no questions asked.

But despite his certainty, it wasn't exactly that way. Yes, some of the kids – the guys anyway – smiled sideways at me and then looked me up and down to determine (I assume) what they had somehow missed. The girl's reactions were less generous. Many of them avoided looking at me at all, some nervously glancing towards the front of the tunnel where Chloe and her friends were standing just outside.

Rob stepped out of the tunnel first and I was still partially hidden by the crowd. I heard Chloe say hello to him – a little curt maybe – but friendly enough. And then she saw me, and I could tell by her face that she hadn't been warned. She looked at us and then Rob's hand on my forearm. The crowd went quiet.

"Seriously?" she said – her eyebrows lifted, and her mouth held slightly open at the end of the word.

"Back off, Chloe."

"Fuck you, Rob."

"Look, don't start. We're leaving."

"We?"

"C'mon Mia," Rob grasped my upper arm protectively and we started walking. Something wet hit my back – someone's beer.

"Sophomore slut," one of Chloe's friends called out.

On the walk back to my house Rob asked me if I was okay about five times. He also kind of went off about Chloe. He said she acted like she owned him and even called her a buzz-wrecking bitch which was, well…wow. When we got to the front door he finally relaxed a bit.

"You're sure you're okay?"

I nodded.

"Can I kiss you goodnight?"

I smiled at his formality. It was sweet the way he was trying to make me feel better. But truth be told, I didn't feel bad. I was still kind of high, and the implications of what had just happened hadn't sunk in. I mean I knew Chloe was mad at Rob, but I wasn't quite grasping how big a deal it all was. All I knew at that moment was that I had just had the most exciting night of my life and now I was finally alone with Rob and I didn't want to talk about Chloe anymore.

I put my arms around Rob's neck and moved closer to him. We started kissing but it wasn't like before. Rob seemed tentative.

After a minute or two, Rob gently pulled my arms off his shoulders.

"You should go in," he said.

I laughed thinking he was being cute – pretending it was a real date and he was dropping me off. When he didn't laugh with me, I suddenly realized what was going on.

"Are you going back?" I asked, trying not to sound as hurt and surprised as I was.

"Uh, yeah. It's only ten."

"Oh."

"You're not mad, are you?"

"No…….no."

He shrugged. "I'm a senior," he added – as if that explained everything, as if there were some kind of law.

I nodded.

Rob smiled and walked back down the three steps in front of our door. At the same time, a car pulled up to the curb and Jake got out. He looked at Rob as they passed each other on the front path but said nothing. When he got to where I was standing, he stopped.

"Is the door locked or something?"

"Oh… I don't know." I turned and tried it. It swung open into the darkened foyer of my house. I didn't move so Jake pushed past me. When I turned back around, Rob was already halfway down the street.

With no other choice, I followed Jake inside. At this moment, you would think I'd be nervous about facing my parents. I mean I had never had a real drink before let alone smoked pot. My sweater (Stephanie's sweater) was still damp and probably reeked of beer. But the fact was, I wasn't thinking about my parents at all. I was too busy trying to figure out what had just happened with Rob. Had I done something wrong? Said something stupid?

I understood that Rob didn't have any obligations to me or any-thing. And he could do whatever he wanted. But I just thought… or I figured that when you ask someone to go somewhere with you – like to a bonfire – it's was because you wanted to be with that person. So why had Rob gone back to the tunnel?

CHAPTER 11

Home Alone

October 25ᵗʰ continued

I stepped into the foyer, wishing more than anything that I could just sneak upstairs and be alone with my Obsessive Repulsive Disorder thoughts, but there was just no way. If I didn't go in and announce that I was home like I normally do, my parents would start asking questions.

I smoothed my hair, gritted my teeth into a cheerful smile and headed into the family room. My parents were sitting on the couch watching some crime drama, an open box of pizza and two empty wine glasses sat on the coffee table in front of them. Jake was standing by the side of the couch, already halfway through a slice of pizza. I stepped into the room and stood as close to the door as I could without looking suspicious.

"Hi, honey," Mom said.

"Hey, Mom."

"Did you have a good time?"

"Yeah."

"Did you two come home together?" She asked glancing at Jake.

"Yup," Jake said, without even hesitating.

I looked at him. He looked back at me – no expression.

"Do you want some pizza? It's a little cold," My mother asked.

I was dying for some pizza. "No thanks."

"Who smells like beer?" My father asked.

Shit. Shit. Shit. "I think it's me," I said.

My father raised his eyebrows.

"I think someone spilled on me." I said turning around to show them and trying to look over my shoulder to see my back.

"Oh no," my mother said. "Is that Stephanie's sweater?"

I nodded.

"I didn't know they served beer at the bonfire?" My father said.

"They don't," Jake replied, "but some of the older kids sneak it in."

I looked at Jake again. He shrugged.

"Do they?" my father asked, looking at Jake suspiciously.

"Oh, yeah, lots of people bring beer," I said trying to sound casual about it.

"Well, just so we're clear," my Dad said, still looking at Jake, "underage drinking is not allowed in this house."

My mother sighed. "They know that, Ray," she said, with an eye roll. Then to me she said, "Go, get changed and bring the sweater down. I'll bring it to the dry cleaners in the morning."

"Thanks mom."

"Sure, sweetie."

And that was it. I couldn't believe my luck. Not only had escaped getting in trouble but I was also going to get Stephanie's sweater cleaned. All thanks to Jake. Go figure. And I was so sure he looked mad when he saw me and Rob at the bonfire. Turns out he was going to keep our secret. Maybe somewhere inside the new, douchebag Jake was the old, nice Jake trying to get out.

Once I was finally alone in my room however, the relief of not getting in trouble wore off almost instantly. I was right back to obsessing about Rob. What was he doing? Was he with Chloe? I spent more than an hour pacing my room trying to come up with a reason to text Rob. I was actually wishing for something to happen to his mom – something good preferably – like her waking up or something. I wished this not because I was a good, caring person but because it would have given me a legitimate reason to interrupt his night. No such luck.

At a little past midnight, I heard the front door open and close. Rob. I quickly turned my lights off. I didn't want him to think I was waiting up for him. Then I listened as he made his way through the house; the refrigerator door, the small TV in the kitchen – sports channel. Then, eventually the stairs, the bathroom, then past my room – not even a pause – and into his (my old) bedroom down the hall.

Let me say for the record that obsessing sucks.

CHAPTER 12

Luck

October 26th

The next morning, I tried unsuccessfully to sleep in. Awake as I was, I wasn't ready to face anyone. No, I had a better idea. I thought it might be super fun to just stay in my room and obsess some more. I spent the morning with a book on my lap, fixated on the noises in the hallway, trying to discern if any of them were Rob. At about eleven-thirty, there was a tap on my door and my heart just about jumped out of my chest. It was only my mom asking if I wanted to go to the hospital with her to see Mrs. Gerber-Starr. I got up and got dressed.

On the way over, my mother told me there was an incident at the high school after the bonfire. Someone had dumped all the trash cans from the food tent all over the parking lot. My mom asked me if I knew anything about it, which I didn't. Then she asked me if I had been with Jake most of the night. Definitely not. She didn't say, but it was pretty clear she thought Jake might have had something to do with those trash cans. That fucking kid, and just when I thought he might not be an asshole.

We got to the hospital around lunch time and it turned out we were just in time to catch Rob, Jake, and their father walking out of Mrs. Gerber-Starr's room. I don't know why I was surprised – I should have figured they were there. I knew Mr. Starr was in town for a few days. And maybe, in the back of my mind, I was hoping they would be. As we walked up to them my heart went at it again – pounding so hard I felt short of breath. *God Mia, get a grip!*

My mother and Mr. Starr spoke for a few minutes before we went in. Apparently, Mrs. Starr's condition had continued to improve. The doctor explained that she was now somewhere between an 8 and a 9 on the Glasgow coma scale. It was weird to think that only two weeks before, I hadn't even known what that was. But now, I felt like I knew everything about comas. For example, I could tell you that a full-on coma – severe brain damage – was considered a 3 or less. A normal, non-comatose person would be a 15 – eye response of 4, a verbal response of 5, and a motor skills response of 6. Mrs. Gerber-Starr's scores were 2, 1 and 3 in that order. In other words, she opened her eyes sometimes, reacted to pain (like when they changed the needle of her IV) and hadn't spoken except to occasionally murmur incoherently. It wasn't much, but according to Mr. Starr; the doctors were pleased.

I kind of hung back behind my mother trying to avoid talking to Rob. But I needn't have worried. He made zero attempt to even look at me.

After several minutes, Mr. Starr announced they were going to get some lunch and would be back in a half hour or so. I looked at Rob who was zipping up his jacket to leave, and I was suddenly annoyed. I mean, I know he was focused on his mom – he *should* be thinking about his mom. It would be weird if he *wasn't* thinking about his mom. But I just couldn't process it. How could he just stand there and ignore me – ignore the fact that we were making out not even fourteen hours ago? Didn't he realize I was freaking out? Hell, if my emotions could make noise, they would have shattered glass.

I didn't know much about guys then, not that I know that much about them now but, at that point, I'd never gone out on a date or even hung out with a lot of guys before. I didn't have any brothers, so I totally didn't understand that guys could be different from girls – that they were wired differently or raised differently or something. In other words, Rob didn't have a clue what was going on in my head. He probably thought everything was fine, and why wouldn't he? I told him I wasn't mad that he went back to the bonfire, and well, that was the end of it for him. Turns out guys believe you when you say stuff like that. Don't say you haven't been warned.

Despite what the doctors said, Mrs. Starr didn't look much better to me. Her skin was papery and her blonde hair was dull – some of her natural brown and a few gray roots having grown in. My mother's eyes filled with tears as she balanced herself on the side of the bed and took her friend's hand. Then she started talking quietly to Mrs. G-S as if Mrs. G-S could hear her.

"Hello Madeline, dear," she said. "How are you? Bill and the boys were just here to see you. Did I tell you how much I love having the boys at my house? They're such good boys – so polite and mature. And they eat! Oh my, I can't believe how much they eat! It so satisfying to watch them. The girls eat like birds. Rachel and Hallie are still so little so of course they don't eat anything, and Mia has stopped eating altogether, from what I can tell. It's the age though – you know, when they start to think about boys…"

"Mom, I'm right here," I said. I mean seriously. The woman has no concept of privacy.

My mother continued talking to Mrs. G-S without looking up. "The doctors say you're getting better, sweetie, which is such wonderful news. I think the boys miss you… especially Jake. And well, selfishly, I really hope you'll be well enough to help me organize the Winter Wish event. It won't be the same without you. I'll be stuck doing the décor with Eloise Evens, and you know how she loves brights. That's fine for the Spring Fling but is just all wrong in the middle of winter. Don't you think?"

"Calista?" Mrs. Gerber-Starr whispered.

My mother started at the word. We looked at each other for a half of a second.

"Yes, Madeline, I'm right here," my mother replied then she turned to me, "Mia, go get…", she started to say but I was already halfway out the door.

I ran as fast as I could down the stairs to the lobby and then out into the parking lot. Mr. Starr was backing his silver BMW out of a corner spot when I ran up. I could barely catch my breath.

"She spoke," I gasped into his partly open window.

Mr. Starr stopped the car halfway out of the parking spot and got out. He ran back into the hospital with the boys at his heels.

I grabbed the keys from the car, shut the door, and followed them back inside – walking. I wasn't sure if it was my place to rush back. When I got to the room, I hesitated just outside the door and peaked in. Mr. Starr was sitting on the bed where my mother had been. Mrs. G-S appeared to be asleep again. The doctor was there talking quietly to my mother. I looked at Rob. He was beaming – streaks of tears on his cheeks. When he saw me, he slipped out into the hall and when he was sure no one was paying attention, he grabbed me, picked me up, and spun me around.

"It's you," he whispered. "You're good luck."

And that was that. I was happy again. I guess that's how it works when something important happens like Rob's mom waking up. Everything seems clearer. I mean, what was the big deal anyway? So, he'd gone back to hang out with his friends? So what? Why had I gotten so freaked out? Hadn't he taken me to the tunnel with him?

Kissed me in front of a bunch of people? Held my hand…okay, my arm… in front of Chloe?

That night we had a huge dinner at our house. Everyone was in a great mood, even though we were all really tired and the doctors had made it clear that Mrs. G-S had a long way to go before she was fully recovered. I had a particularly good time because A) Mr. Starr insisted on giving me a ridiculous amount of money for tutoring Rob, who had miraculously managed to get an eighty-three on his Trig test. And B) because Rob sat across from me and I could tell he was looking at me. He even winked when he thought no one was watching. I'm pretty sure Jake caught it because he was watching us the whole time, although he was trying to pretend he wasn't. Luckily, nobody else seemed to notice.

On Sunday, instead of visiting Mrs. Gerber-Starr, my mother took me and Hallie to the mall. I think she wanted to give Bill and the kids some family time with Mrs. G-S.

Rob wasn't home when we got back. He had gone out with his friends, which of course he had every right to do. I mean if we lived in different houses, I wouldn't have the slightest idea what he was doing or where he was going, and I knew I'd be better off if I could just think of it that way.

But (thanks to my good friend ORD) questions kept popping into my mind. Why did it seem like Rob really liked me one minute but barely noticed me the next? And, what was it going to be like at school the next day? How was I supposed to act? Would he want me to hang out with him and his friends? Kiss him if I saw him in the hall? I didn't know the first thing about being someone's girlfriend – not that I was officially Rob's girlfriend, I mean that was almost too much to even consider – but I was his *something*, …right?

Ellsworth High School Case #1141
Transcript of interview: March 21
Student: Mia Morgan
Counselor: Dr. Janis Dubrovski

Dr. Dubrovski: *I'm a bit confused here, Mia. Why would three popular kids- two boys and a girl – want to post pictures like this?*

Mia Morgan: *I ... I don't know. Maybe they thought it would be funny.*

Dr. Dubrovski: *Maybe. I know kids can be cruel. I've certainly seen it before. But this strikes me as a bit extreme just for a laugh. It seems so carefully orchestrated; even premeditated. Certainly, you must have thought about this. You must have some theory as to why they did this to you...why you were singled out.*

Mia Morgan: *I guess.*

Dr. Dubrovski: *And?*

Mia Morgan: *And what?*

Dr. Dubrovski: *Can you remember doing something that might have made someone mad? Maybe something you didn't realize you were doing? Start a rumor? Tell a secret? Perhaps there was a boy involved? Maybe you made someone jealous.*

Mia Morgan: *Me?*

CHAPTER 13

No Friends and No "Daz"

October 26th & 27th

So, turns out, I was DEFINITELY NOT Rob's girlfriend. The fact that I'd even imagined…well, it just shows you how clueless I was. But I'm getting ahead of myself here. Let's go back a little, to Sunday night.

After dinner, I decided it was time I told my friends what was going on with me and Rob. I was planning to explain that I hadn't said anything before because I just wasn't sure there was really anything to say.

I'll admit, I was surprised that no one had tried to text me to ask me, but I was so caught up in my own obsession with Rob, I hadn't really thought about it all that hard. I guess I'd sort of figured they were just waiting for me to make the first gesture.

I started with Stephanie, of course, and then Carmen, Angelica, Jenna, and Jonah and by ten o'clock or so, I had texted every one of my friends and no one had answered. It took a while for it to sink in, but I finally realized I was being ghosted by my entire friend group.

As you might imagine, it was awful. My feelings shifted between hurt, (as in how-could-they-just-abandon-me-because-I'd-hung-out-one-night-with-Rob-Starr), to pissed off as in (what-the-hell?). And yes, there was the pact and everything, but really... It was one night; was it really such a big deal? As if any of them would have turned down the opportunity to hang out with Rob Starr (or basically any other popular kid at Ellsworth High School) if they had the chance. Which they didn't. Which was clearly the issue. I went to bed half miserable, half furious and, needless to say, didn't get much sleep.

Because of Mrs. G-S's continued improvement, Rob and Jake, were no longer on a "family crisis schedule" and had left by the time I made it down to the kitchen the next morning. Not that I thought ... I mean I knew Rob had pre-season practice in the mornings, so it wasn't like I thought we were going to be walking to school together or anything. I was fine walking to school alone. It wasn't a big deal. Plenty of kids did it.

But when I stepped outside, I felt naked. Normally Steph and Angelica would be waiting for me on the sidewalk in front of my house. And normally, my mom sent me off with a toasted bagel with butter which the three of us shared on the way, followed by one of Angelica's ever-present wint-o-green Life Savers to counteract the bagel breath. And normally, even though I hadn't realized it until then, I felt safe and protected by my nerdy little group. But things were not normal. No one was waiting for me in front of my house. I stashed my sad, friendless bagel in my backpack.

I had only gone a few steps when I heard someone call my name. Sally Verma.

Sally was a junior who lived just a couple of houses down from me. Even though we were close in age, we'd never become friends. The only thing we had in common – if you could even call it that – was that we were equally unpopular.

Unlike me, who avoided attention whenever possible, Sally was one of those overachiever types. She was on student government and the debate team and had the highest GPA in the junior class. On top of all that she was the secretary of the science club and co-captain of the girl's gymnastics team.

You might think that someone with so many creds and activities would also have a ton of friends, but not Sally. She came on way too hard – bragging about her grades, or some new handbag, or her families vacation house in the DR. She was so annoying kids called her Sally Vermin behind her back. And to make matters worse, she was totally obsessed with the Baditudes. She was so desperate to be one, she even tried out for cheer *three* years in a row (more than twice is just mortifying). Even with her impressive gymnastic skills, it was never going to happen.

Whenever we spoke, which was rarely, she could barely focus, always glancing over my shoulder in search of someone higher on the social food chain. So, you can imagine my surprise when she walked up and fell into step beside me.

"Where are your friends?" Sally asked.

"They went in early for something," I lied.

"Perfect," she replied, looking around to be sure no one was in earshot.

"So…" she leaned in as if we were besties, "are you and Rob Starr a thing?"

"Oh," I said, startled by the directness of her question. "Uh… no…I mean, what do you mean?"

"Cuz everyone is saying you were together at the bonfire." She said the word 'together' slowly to give it emphasis. "But I was texting with Justin McCloud last night, and he told me that Rob said you weren't."

"We were just hanging out," I said, trying to sound nonchalant, though I could feel the blood rushing to my face; my mind whirling with what Rob might have said to Justin about me.

"Well *everyone* is talking about it."

Maybe it was the way she said 'everyone', but it finally hit me. I was, quite possibly, the stupidest person in the world. What had I been thinking? What had I done? Everything Rob Starr did was headline news. Did I really think I could just kiss Rob Starr in public and people would be …okay with it? Happy for me? Holy shit! No wonder my friends weren't talking to me. They were probably just trying to save themselves – trying to get some distance from the social hand grenade I'd lobbed at myself.

"We were just hanging out," I said again, though not even close to convincingly. We turned the corner and headed for the crosswalk. Two sophomore girls were coming towards us from the other direction. "I've got to go," Sally said quickly. "I have a test."

Have you heard the expression 'tip of the iceberg'? Because that was Sally. Nothing I'd experienced before could have prepared me for what it was like in school that day. Sure, in the last few weeks, since the Starrs had moved in, I'd gotten a little taste of what it felt like to be in the spotlight, but it was nothing compared to this. I couldn't have gotten more attention if I had been riding through the halls on Santa's sleigh wearing a see-thru bikini and throwing money.

Everyone stared at me, whispering about me as I walked past, a hand cupped over their mouths like in the movies. A few even pointed. I didn't know how to react except to pretend I didn't notice. But when Stephanie and Carmen walked by me in the hall and purposely didn't look at me, I felt like I might throw up.

At lunch, I ate my cold bagel from breakfast in a bathroom stall, which was both pathetic and disgusting and made worse by the fact that I overheard two Team Hotties talking about me. Note, they entered the bathroom in mid-conversation and exited while still talking so all I got was the middle, but it went something like:

"…in our Art class and she's like… kind of loser-ish. She the one that sits at the table by the windows with those two other girls. She's not that pretty. I mean not a complete barf or anything, but like zero daz." (an Ellsworth word – short for dazzle – made popular by the cheer squad's trophy-winning Razzle Dazzle routine).

"Does she have light brown hair?"

"No, that's her friend. She's got like frizzy dark brown hair and she wears it in a ponytail all the time."

"Oh yeah…I think I know who she is…"

"Well anyway, that's the girl he's been staying with since his mom's accident. I heard she snuck into his room the night he moved in and like, tried to give him a blow job."

"What? No way! If it's the girl I think you mean, that did *not* happen. That girl has never even *kissed* a boy. I mean, has she even gone through puberty yet? Besides, I don't care how nerdy you are, no one is that stupid. No one in their right mind would go after Rob Starr."

"Yeah, you're probably right. Justin says nothing happened. Rob was just being nice – letting her hang out with them, you know, because he's staying with her fam…"

They walked out at that point and I don't know how long I sat there, on the edge of that toilet seat, trying to process all the insults I had just heard about myself. It was stunning to hear people talk about you – like really talk about you – without any thought of sparing your feelings. It hurt for sure, but it was also weirdly freeing. I now knew what other people said about me and while it wasn't very flattering, the fact was, it was all kind of accurate. I was kind of loser. My hair was frizzy. And I definitely didn't have "daz".

No, it wasn't the insults that bothered me. The part that really bugged me – the part that sent my ORD into the stratosphere – was the part about Justin saying that nothing happened. I mean he was *there*. He *knew* something happened. But hadn't Sally Verma said the same thing? Well almost the same. She'd said that Rob *told* Justin nothing happened. Which was even worse – obviously.

On top of everything else, I got a text – from my mother – that Rob had to cancel his Trig study session with me for that afternoon. According to her, he said something about basketball. Then from practice he'd have to go see his mom, of course. I desperately wanted to know every detail of their conversation but there was just no way to ask without making her suspicious.

After lunch I had Art and, of course, I had completely forgotten I was supposed to have a subject for our portrait drawing project. We were supposed to pick someone we admired. I hadn't even thought about it. And, as my luck was going, Mrs. James called on me first. I hesitated. From the other side of the room someone called out in a high, squeaky voice, "Rob Starr. He's so dreamy". Everyone laughed. For a second, I thought it might have been Jake, but when I glanced over at him, he was looking down at his hands as if he were as embarrassed as I was. I ended up picking my mom. Lame, I know.

When I got home that afternoon, no one was there but Jake – the last person I wanted to see. We ran into each other in the kitchen, both fixing ourselves a snack. We said nothing, as usual, but when he picked up his cereal bowl to leave, he stopped.

"Are you okay" he asked, not quite looking in my direction.

"What? Yes. Fine." I answered curtly and pushed past him to go upstairs. Things were clearly pretty bad if Jake thought he had to be nice to me.

When I got to my room, I couldn't concentrate on anything. I basically sat on my bed with my homework in front of me and listened for Rob to get home from practice, which he did – only to turn around and head out to the hospital, as planned. Feeling very lonely and more than a little freaked out, I kept randomly texting my friends in hopes that one of them might answer. Angela did start to text back at one point – I saw the little dots appear on my screen indicating she was typing – but then they stopped and there was nothing.

Hours went by. I checked my phone about a million times – not a single text or pic from anyone. I can't tell you how weird it feels to not get any messages – nothing at all. I felt almost desperately alone. Was I dreaming? Was I dead?

Rob came in around ten, but he didn't come upstairs. I waited. I laid as still as I could, so I could hear better but all I could make out was the sound of the TV. He must have fallen asleep watching the sports channel. I finally fell asleep at around one.

On Tuesday, I signed up for Mr. Hansell's extra credit Trig lunch period because at least it was better than eating lunch in the bathroom. However, by Tuesday night I was climbing out of my skin. I had seen Rob in the hall that afternoon, but he didn't see me. He seemed perfectly normal. Laughing, tossing a basketball around with his friends. Why was Rob's life going on as if nothing happened and my life was completely over?

If you're wondering, the answer is yes, of course I thought about texting him. I was *obsessing* about it. But I kept thinking, what if I text him and he doesn't text me back? What then? Then I'd know for sure that he didn't like me – that he never had – and was probably embarrassed about what happened. Or worse, maybe he'd text me back to say he'd gotten back together with Chloe and he'd just forgotten to tell me because I just didn't matter enough for him to remember.

Since I clearly wasn't ready to face that possible (probable) reality. I would not text him. I would continue to hold onto hope as tightly as I could – playing again and again in my head how he'd spun me around and whispered 'you're good luck' in my ear.

CHAPTER 14

No Mr. Darcy

October 30ᵗʰ & 31ˢᵗ

By Thursday, people seemed to have calmed down, at least somewhat, about the whole bonfire thing. But let me pause for a second and say that even though I wrote, "By Thursday" as if time just floated by between Tuesday night and Thursday, I want to be clear. IT HADN'T.

However, I promised to skip over the psycho-boring parts, so as I was saying, by Thursday, things had calmed down a bit. Most of the school had lost interest in me, with the exception of my friends who were still actively *not* talking to me even though I had texted them each a dozen times and the Baditudes whom, despite my best efforts, could not be one hundred percent avoided. Whenever I passed one of them, I could feel them looking at me. They didn't say anything, thankfully, but I think one of them hissed at me outside the girl's locker room – yup, hissed – although I can't be sure.

Thursday still managed to suck, however. Mostly because I still hadn't really talked to Rob (I did see him once in the kitchen before school on Wednesday and he said, "Morning Mia" and I said "Hi"). And because I'd taken the AP Bio test the day before, which I had barely studied for, and got a seventy-four which was my worst grade on an exam since seventh grade English when I got a seventy-one on the To Kill a Mockingbird final because I was out with strep throat for almost two weeks. I knew I should have cared more about that seventy-four, and had it been a couple of weeks prior, I probably would have lost my mind. But I was so caught up in my little drama, it barely registered.

At lunch on Friday, I sat with Sally Verma and her (only) friend Veronica – a sometimes HB&P – who was only slightly more popular than Sally and only because she had a nice car. Like everyone else in school, they spent the period discussing their costumes for the Halloween Haunt which was happening that night. They were going as the creepy twins from The Shining – which was a very cool costume idea, however totally unimportant to my story – but just in case you were wondering.

Halloween in Ellsworth was a very big deal – maybe even bigger than Christmas. Okay, not as big as Christmas, but seriously big. People went all-out with the decorations – yards were transformed into cemeteries; front doors were rigged to unleash ghosts from the rooftops and pumpkin carving had become a veritable art form. But the single biggest deal on Halloween was the Halloween Haunt.

The Haunt was a fund raiser (this was Ellsworth after all) hosted every year by the senior class and the PTA. There was a haunted maze inside the school (the main attraction), plus a big tent in the parking lot with cookies and caramel apples and cider where everyone hung out. The goal was to raise money for the high school library, and because of that, The Haunt always had a book theme. This basically meant that you didn't just wear ordinary Halloween costumes, you had to dress up as characters from a book.

I know it sounds dorky, but it was really sort of fun. And when you think about it, there are books about pretty much everything, so you could make any costume fit the theme if you tried hard enough.

One of the main organizers of the event was (not surprisingly) my very own mother, the two-time PTA president and event co-ordinator extraordinaire, Command Central Calista. And because of that, the Morgan family (my family, in case you forgot my last name) went hard on the costume thing.

Each year we'd pick a book and dress up as a family. Last year it was Dad's turn to choose. We went as The Stark family from Game of Thrones (Book 1, to be specific). Dad went as Ned (and spoiler alert here), he even had a post-beheading scar around his neck in honor of Halloween. My mother went as Catherine, me as Sansa and Hallie as Arya. We even borrowed the neighbor's German Shepherds to stand in as wolves. And it was fun because, well, I was still young enough and invisible enough and geeky enough that no one really cared what I did. Besides, most of my friends were dressed up with their geeky families too.

But not this year. This year I was a sophomore and me and my geeky friends had been planning to go, without our families, as the tributes from the Hunger Games, (total geek-fun). I imagined this was still their plan, but I'd been dropped from that group chat days ago. Not that it mattered. My mother had decided we were going together as a family – this one last time – to show her "community spirit." But I suspected it was more because she wanted one last shot at the family costume contest, which we'd lost to the Evans's every year for the last five years.

I couldn't seem to make her understand how the whole family-costume thing was just totally uncool at my age. "You can just hang out with your friends later," she'd said in that clueless way parents have, as if they themselves were never teenagers.

To my further embarrassment, my mother had invited Rob, Jake, and Rachel to join us in dressing up (Pride and Prejudice – Mom's choice). Rachel was totally into it – she really was a cute kid. However, to absolutely no one's surprise on earth, both Rob and Jake said they'd already made other plans. I was hugely relieved of course. It would just be too weird; Rob dressed up as the gorgeous yet brooding Mr. Darcy, me as Elizabeth Bennet, his love interest. Can you picture it? Yeah, me neither.

The basketball team, football team and the cheerleaders were going as zombies from The Walking Dead. And if you aren't yet feeling the full extent of my misery, keep in mind that while Chloe and the other cheer girls would be wearing shredded-up versions of their already tiny clothing – strategically ripped to expose even more of their perfect bodies, I would be in an early eighteenth century gown with lace up boots and a bonnet. A f-ing bonnet.

CHAPTER 15

Bonnets Suck

October 31ˢᵗ

So about six hours later, there I was in the back seat of my parent's SUV, dressed like Elizabeth Bennet and squeezed in next to Rachel and Hallie (Lydia and Kitty Bennet) who were bouncing around like the incredibly irritating fourth graders they were. The only good news was that my costume wasn't as totally lame as I thought it was going to be. It was a creamy-gold silky material and it had this sort of half corset thing sewn into the dress that squashed my boobs from the bottom, pushing them up and making it look like I had some pretty serious cleavage, which I didn't. Apparently, people in the eighteenth century were very into cleavage – who knew?

But don't think that my totally loser costume issues were solved just because I was showing a little top boob. Keep in mind I still had to wear the bonnet and I was out for the evening with my family who were also dressed like "ye olde" English country idiots.

We got to the event early (of course), and after stopping for our photo in front of the costume judges, Hallie, Rachel, and I made our way to the haunted maze. Hallie and Rachel were a bit nervous, the maze is infamously scary especially for young kids. It's always very dark and draped with white sheets and there are fog machines and weird noises. The seniors dress up and act out all sorts of bloody (red paint) murder scenes and pop out at you when you walk by. And if I had been going through with my friends, say Stephanie and Jenna, they would have really tried to freak us out. But since I had younger kids with me, most of the kids were keeping it tame. At least until we got to the science lab. Suddenly this zombie football player pops out at us and really frightens Rachel and Hallie, which would have been fine – fun even – if he had left it at one big scare. But then he started following us.

At first, I couldn't tell who it is because he had all this gray makeup on his face, and it was seriously dark in there. One of his arms was tucked inside his shirt and there was a fake stuffed arm sort of swinging by his side. He didn't talk and was just sort of hanging back a few steps behind us breathing really loudly and well, it was creepy.

I wasn't really scared because I knew it was just some asshole jock, but he was starting to upset Hallie who didn't like spooky stuff in the first place and who had only agreed to go through the haunted maze because I had promised her it wouldn't be that bad.

I told him to cut it out a couple of times and finally, he disappeared, only to pop out at us again in the next room which really freaked Hallie out.

"Hey, I told you that's enough," I said.

"Sorry," he answered in this this not very convincing spooky voice, "but I'm sooooo very hungry. I think I must eat you."

"Seriously Justin," I said, because now I could tell by the voice that it was Justin McCloud (who was, as you might guess, just about the last person in the world I wanted to see), "You're scaring them."

"That's the whole idea, M'lady," he said, bowing to me (I figured he was using the M'lady stuff because of my costume). Anyway, he sounded buzzed which wasn't great news considering he was an idiot even when he was sober.

"I'm not scared," said Hallie even though she was practically crying.

"Perhaps if you'll allow me just a little snack," he said leering at my partially exposed boobs, "I'll let the children go."

"Uh...no," I said. "Come on girls, let's go."

"I'll show you the way, M'ladies," Justin said, stepping closer to us, "but how about a little bite first?" he added, breathing too close to my face.

I started to back away from him but with his one free arm he grabbed me and somehow managed to throw me over his shoulder. I'm sure he thought he was being funny, and if I had been with Stephanie and Jenna all three of us would have probably shrieked with delight. But I was with Hallie and Rachel. Hallie burst into tears and started screaming "Mom" at the top of her lungs. This freaked Rachel out and she burst into tears as well. Finally, Justin put me down, but it was too late.

Someone turned the lights on, and I managed get the girls outside with the help of Marissa DiMartino and Katie Griggs (two HB&Ps who, for some reason – probably because they recognized Rachel as Rob's sister – decided to be human beings). I barely took the time to thank them however because I was so completely mortified at having drawn so much attention to my bonnet-wearing-loser-virgin self. I quickly dragged Hallie and Rachel to the food tent and shoved caramel apples at them.

Then I heard Rob. "What the hell did you do?" he yelled. I turned to see him standing several feet away from me. He was dressed as a basketball zombie and was shouting in football zombie Justin's face. "Are you a fucking idiot or something?"

"What the hell?" Justin shouted back. "What do I know about little kids?"

"Fuck, man!" Rob said shaking his head with exasperation. He turned away from Justin and headed towards us. When he walked past me, he gave me only the briefest glance, from which I got the message 'you should have been watching out for my sister instead of flirting with my asshole friend' (yes, all that in one look). Which kind of threw me because it was totally unfair. He went directly to Rachel.

"Are you okay, Rach?"

She nodded.

"You sure?"

She nodded again, but the tears were back in her eyes. "I don't like zombies," she said.

Rob nodded. "Okay, well me neither... I was just about to take this stuff off." He lifted his shirt – revealing his perfect stomach which really has nothing to do with the story – and swiped the fabric across his face so some of the makeup was wiped away. "See? Just makeup."

Rachel nodded again.

"You're okay," he said, pushing her bangs away from her forehead. "Nothing happened." He was kneeling now, so they were face to face. "It was just stupid Justin. You know Justin from the team, right?"

Rachel nodded and looked cautiously over Rob's shoulder at Justin who was across the parking lot talking to some other kids.

Rob tugged at her bonnet string, and I suddenly realized I was still wearing mine. Did I mention it was grandma's-curtains yellow with tiny pink rose buds? Not that there was a color or pattern that could have made it cool.

Could this night get any worse? And by the way, the answer to that seemingly rhetorical question is yes, yes it could. I quickly slid the bonnet back from my forehead and tried to fluff up my hair a little.

"I have to go back inside for a few more minutes," Rob said

Rob turned to me. "Mia, would you mind keeping an eye on Rachel until I get back?" Again, clearly suggesting by his tone that I was somehow shirking this responsibility.

"Of course not."

So, okay, of course I didn't mind. But I did kind of mind being silently accused of something I didn't do. And by the way, it might have been nice if he had asked me or Hallie if we were okay. And sure, I get it, he was worried about Rachel, which was super sweet. Or it would have been super sweet if he had actually come back in a couple of minutes like he told her he would. But he didn't. And I don't mean that he took a long time to come back, I mean he just didn't.

My father found us about a half hour after the incident – Rob still not back – and took the girls off trick-or-treating. I stayed behind, telling him I was going to find my friends, but the truth was that I was waiting for Rob. At this point I still thought he might come back, and I didn't want him to wonder where we had gone. And, strangely enough, I felt guilty even though I hadn't done anything wrong. You would think I would just leave since he'd been such an asshole about the Rachel thing, but I was willing to let it go for even a few minutes of his time. I know. I know. It's pathetic.

So, as I was saying, Rob didn't come back. And he really should have because as far as he knew, Rachel was waiting for him. And what about me? I was waiting there too, feeling totally awkward, practically hiding behind a tent flap trying to keep people from noticing the fact that I was completely alone. And okay he couldn't have known that, but it was still starting to piss me off (I know, *finally,* right?). I mean not only was he currently acting like a jerk but he had completely ignored me the whole week and it had been a crappy, horrible, confusing, exhausting week; a none-of-my-friends-are-speaking-to-me, I-got-a-seventy-four-on-my-AP-Bio-test and the-popular-kids-are-hissing-at-me-in-the-halls kind of a week. And I just didn't know what I'd done wrong. Why wouldn't he just talk to me?

After a total of one hour and nine minutes of waiting, I gave up hope. Besides, I was becoming more and more conspicuous as the crowd began to thin. My only choice was to find my mother and get out of there. I headed back towards the exit where a lot of the adults had gathered waiting for their kids to emerge from the maze. As I rounded the corner of the building, I heard some shouting and cheering as another group successfully "made it out alive." Among the "survivors" was Rob, most of his zombie makeup had been smeared away and his face was sort of shiny and gray in the building's flood lights. For the first time – maybe ever in his life – he didn't look that great. It might have had something to do with the fact that he was carrying Samantha Hernandez on his shoulders – a super curvy and super popular senior (a core member of the Heam Totties) – who was dressed as what could only be described as the stripper version of Pippi Longstocking. Her arms were raised over her head in glorious triumph – a raggedy vest flapping open to reveal her big bouncing boobs, which were barely hanging on to the flimsy white tube top she wore underneath.

I stopped in my tracks. They were coming towards me and there was nowhere for me to go. Rob had a good hold on Samantha's bare legs – from where I stood, I was close enough to see his fingers pressing into her skin – and he was sort of jogging, leading a bunch of other kids in a victory lap for the crowd. He shouted something – a kind of a triumphant howl – then turned with his mouth still open and bit the inside of Samantha's abundant thigh – growling and shaking his head as if he were an animal…or a zombie, I suppose. She screamed and teasingly smacked him on the top of his head.

And then, for no reason at all, he looked right at me as if he knew I was going to be standing there – his teeth still clenched on Samantha's flesh. When our eyes met, I flinched as though I'd been slapped.

Rob turned away and finished his lap, disappearing into the small crowd. I stood there, stunned. Was Rob with Samantha Hernandez? I didn't know what to do. I was going to throw up.

I had to get out of there. I had to move. I turned around and started pushing back through the crowd. There were people everywhere – trick-or-treaters, Gandalf, Alice in Wonderland, parents, zombies, The Cat in The Hat, Oompa Loompas. For a moment, I locked eyes with Carmen. She was standing with Jonah and Stephanie near the cider table, and I could instantly tell that she'd been watching me. She'd seen me watching Rob. There was pity in her face and not in a mean way, in a kind of friend-who-might-actually-care way, but it wasn't enough to stop me. Once I broke free of the crowd, I ran – all twelve blocks, to my house, in my stupid Elizabeth Bennet shoes, with the stupid bonnet strings practically strangling me the entire way.

CHAPTER 16

What Text?

*October 31*ˢᵗ *continued*

When I got home, I found Rachel and Hallie sitting on the floor of the family room with the booty from their Halloween bags piled high beside them. They were deep in trade negotiations – two chocolate kisses for one peanut butter cup – the trauma of the haunted maze cured by large doses of chocolate and caramel. I envied them.

My parents were in the kitchen, still in costume, drinking tea and eating the candy rejects (anything with coconut and those weird Mary Jane things – where do people even buy those?). I think they were sort of flirting with each other, which was kind of adorable and disgusting at the same time. At least I managed to get upstairs without having to say much.

Once I was back to being Mia, I found myself waiting for Rob again. He came in about an hour later. He came upstairs almost immediately and went into the bathroom to take a shower.

A few moments later, I heard Jake come home and climb the stairs two at a time. He went directly into the bathroom and said something to Rob. I couldn't hear what they were saying but it sounded like they were arguing. They fought a lot, which I guess was normal for brothers. The only words I could make out were at the end of the encounter when Jake had opened the door again to leave – "Why are you always such a dick?" (from Jake) and "Piss off!" (from Rob).

I heard the shower go off, and a minute later that there was a knock on my door. Although this was exactly what I'd been hoping for, when the knock came, I wasn't sure what to do. I quickly paused the show I'd been fake-watching on my computer and pulled the elastic out of my hair, trying unsuccessfully to smooth down the frizz around my face.

I opened the door a crack. It was Rob. He was wearing an old-looking college t-shirt and sweatpants. His hair was wet, and his skin was clean but there was still some residual black zombie makeup smudged around his eyes, making them look grey and wolfish and, of course, totally, ridiculously gorgeous.

"Let me in."

"What do you want?"

"To talk."

"What about?"

"Come on Mia. I want to talk about tonight."

"What about it?" I said stepping back a bit, so he could push the door open and step into the room.

"Well for starters, you looked really pretty in your costume," he said.

"Apparently not pretty enough," I replied, surprising myself.

Rob was suddenly irritated.

"What did you expect? Your parents were there."

"I don't know what I expected. It just didn't seem like…"

"Nothing happened with me and Sam if that's what you think," Rob interrupted. "She's just a friend. We were all just goofing around. And it's like I told you in my text. We have to act like nothing is going on with us."

Text? What text?

"And you know as well as I do that Chloe and her bitchy friends would go psycho if they thought something... You remember how they were at the bonfire?"

Okay, so, he had a point there. Even if Chloe was like thirty and married and had kids, she would probably put a hit out on anyone who was hooking up with Rob. But more importantly, what text?

Rob continued. "She'd probably tell your parents, or she'd make someone else tell them and they'd freak out. I mean c'mon; if you were a dad, would you want some kid living in your house who's hooking up with your daughter? They'd kick me out in a heartbeat."

Mmmm. Another good point but still, there was NO TEXT. And I'd been a crazy ORD psycho for too many hours to just go along with this.

"And when you didn't text me back, I guess I thought, I mean I don't know what I thought..."

I took a deep breath. "I don't think we should do this anymore," I said – surprising myself yet again.

"What? Why?"

"I don't know...it's just...I mean...I understand. I'm a sophomore and you're a senior... and Chloe and your mom and everything... and like you said, my parents would freak out if they found out. I don't know...it's fine. I mean, I get it. I do. I get it."

Rob looked at me for what seemed like a full minute. He looked sad or hurt and maybe a little angry.

"No," he said finally.

I took a sharp breath in, getting ready to repeat my case but before I could talk, Rob reached out and grabbed the waistband of my pajama pants in his fist and tugged me towards him. "No," he said again. "They don't get to win. We get to win." Then he kissed me, and it was amazing – made even more intense because we were both naked under our clothes – of course everyone is naked under their clothes, but you know what I mean – no underwear. After a minute or so I managed to push him away.

"The door is open," I said.

"So, let's close it," Rob said.

"Are you crazy? My parents…"

"What about them? They won't know. They would never think…"

"What? They would never think what? That you would be in my room? That you would be interested in me?"

"That is *not* what I was going to say."

I stepped back. It took actual, physical effort.

"You should go," I whispered.

"Please don't do this Mia. I *am* interested in you. I mean, I'm here aren't I? I could be out with my friends." He sounded frustrated or maybe annoyed.

"Well you don't have to do me any favors." My voice shook.

"C'mon Mia, don't be like this." Rob reached for me again, but I backed away.

"Don't."

Rob looked at me. His expression said, 'Are you sure that's what you want?'

We stood there. Neither one of us saying anything.

"Okay," Rob said eventually. He shrugged and shook his head and ran his hand through his wet hair. "Okay," he said again. And then he left the room. And I felt like someone had just punched me in the stomach. And I know, I know, I was the one who had just broken it off with him – I mean assuming you could even call it that because, if you really thought about it, it was more like I was breaking it off on his behalf. Because really, WHAT TEXT? And still, I was devastated.

CHAPTER 17

Really Good Friends

November 1ˢᵗ

The next day was Saturday. I woke up to my phone buzzing on the bed beside my pillow. It was raining outside; miserable and raw, which was perfect because it totally matched my mood. I picked up my phone. It was a text from Rob:

> *Why you are being like this? Last night at the haunt I was just hanging out with my friends and trying to take my mind off all the shit I'm dealing with and I really thought that you would understand that. I thought you were different and that you really understood me. And if you're pissed about the Samantha thing well that's totally history and I don't know what I can do about that because like I said, we're just friends and I'm not into her. I'm into you.*

I read the message again. And while I was partly thrilled, I was also partly not. I was so confused; I honestly didn't know how to feel.

Maybe I was crazy (lately, for sure) or uncool (already established) or old-fashioned (I never thought so…) but it seemed to me that if you were into somebody, you would act like you were into them. You would text them and send funny pictures and hang out with them. You wouldn't go a whole week barely speaking to them even if you had to hide your relationship from the world. Right? And what about the Samantha part? What did he mean by "that was totally history?" He made it sound like something had happened between them, but when? I thought Rob had only ever been with Chloe. But maybe not. Should I be worried? Upset? Angry?

And did I even have the right to be? I mean, we hadn't really agreed to anything. We hadn't had any official conversation about being a couple or not seeing other people. Nothing even close to that had been discussed. And maybe he was genuinely worried about my parents finding out – or that the Baditudes would harass me. And it was possible that he'd texted me like he said he did, and I just didn't get it for some reason. Shit. Shit. Shit. Shit.

Was he here in the house, I wondered? I texted. I waited, hoping- no – praying that he wasn't. I hadn't slept much. Every time closed my eyes, I pictured Rob's fingers pressing into Samantha Hernandez's thighs. The lack of sleep combined with all the crying left me looking like a puffy, red potato.

Rob's text: I'm with my mom.

Of course. He was with his sick mom. Because he was a normal person doing normal things. Not a total ORD psycho like me.

Me: We should talk

No answer.

No answer.

No answer.

No answer.

Twelve minutes later.

Rob: ok

I took a shower and washed my hair.

About two hours later they came back: Rob, Jake, Rachel, and my mom. I was in the kitchen not doing my homework at the kitchen counter. Rob looked at me and lifted his chin slightly indicating we should go upstairs. I gathered my stuff and made my excuses – too noisy etc. and went up to my room. Five minutes later Rob was at my door.

We didn't talk. We just seriously macked.

Finally, we pulled ourselves apart. It was way too risky in my room, with my parents at home and all.

"I'm sorry," I said.

"It's okay," he said.

I don't remember everything we said but I know he told me he didn't want to be with Samantha or anyone but me. And we agreed we wouldn't see other people. Which was really more like Rob agreeing he wouldn't see other people because it wasn't like I had a long line of suitors or anything. We also agreed it was better if we didn't tell anyone about us. Rob thought the safest thing to do would be to tell people that we'd become good friends. That way we could hang out together and Rob could bring me to parties and stuff but just as friends. And if anyone wondered why he wasn't hooking up with someone, he'd tell them that, because of his mom, he just wasn't into it.

Just a quick note here: if some of you are wondering exactly what I had apologized for – and good question by the way – the answer is, I'm not sure. I just wanted things to be okay with Rob and me and I didn't want to lose him. If that meant saying I'm sorry, even though I really didn't' have anything to be sorry for, then it was worth it. Being with Rob was all I really cared about.

Ellsworth High School Case #1141
Transcript of interview: March 22
Student: Mia Morgan
Counselor: Dr. Janis Dubrovski

Dr. Dubrovski: *What was the significance of the words "little b" on some of the photographs?*
Mia Morgan: *I have no idea.*

CHAPTER 18

Big B Little b

Early November

Rob was having a hard time focusing on the study sheet I'd made for him (yes, it was math-geeky to make a study sheet, but I was getting paid good money). Not that I was doing much better with my Biology homework – which, based on my most recent test scores I think we can all agree, I should have been paying attention to. I was reading about Mendel and Punnett squares and the whole eye color, big B, little b thing – which, by the way, is only partly accurate because there are at least two other genes involved (a fact my teacher, Ms. Howell was not particularly interested in discussing when my (ex) friend Eric brought it up in class). Anyway, Rob kept bumping my knee with his or reaching across me and "accidentally" dropping an eraser down my shirt leading to an PG-rated search for the lost eraser. We lasted about fifteen minutes before we were full-on making out.

After of few minutes, Rob put his hand on my breast. Just FYI, normally I would never call them breasts – just too cheesy-romance-novel for me. I'd call them boobs, or…well that's really it – because I hate the word tits or any of the other words for boobs, but anyway, it seemed sort of goofy to write 'Rob put his hand on my boob… so breast it is, like it or not. Anyway, Rob put his hand there, outside my shirt, and it felt, well, nice, so I didn't stop him. And he, being a guy, took that as the invitation to move on to the next step.

Probably needless to say, Rob was way more experienced at this stuff than I was. He pulled me onto his lap and started to unbutton my shirt. So, you can get the whole picture, I had not planned for any of this and was wearing a striped button down, from the Mia Morgan Invisible Girl Collection, and a plain beige bra. And despite what lingerie makers might have you believe, this didn't seem to be the least bit disappointing to Rob. When my shirt fell open, he paused and admired me – no other way to describe it – running his finger slowly over the exposed skin above my bra line and giving me goosebumps. Then he leaned in and started kissing my shoulder while at the same time sliding his hands around my back to unhook it my bra.

"Wait," I said.

"Mmm?" He murmured. His hands had stopped moving but his mouth was still on the upper part of my chest near my neck.

"It's just…I'm shy, I guess."

He pulled back to look at me. "Why?"

"I don't know, I'm just…"

"Beautiful?"

"Yeah, that's the problem, I'm too beautiful," I said sarcastically… nervously.

Rob reached up and pushed some imaginary hair from my face. "You are beautiful." He kissed me and then slowly moved his hand back down to my breast.

"Wait…" I blurted. I was almost panicked with self-consciousness. What if he thought my mismatched boobs were freaky? "I'm… One's…"

"What? he said casually, "a little smaller than the other. Yeah, I noticed that a while ago."

I looked at him, shocked.

He grinned. "Hey, I'm a guy. I noticed your boobs. What do you want me to say?"

I must have blushed because Rob reached out for my face again. "I think they're perfect... I think you're perfect."

Well, things got pretty steamy after that.

Anyway, at some point my mother came home from the gym and the noise of the kitchen door startled us. We immediately jumped apart and quickly put ourselves in order. Luckily, we were in the dining room which is kind of off the main path of our house, so she didn't catch us doing anything. By the time she got to around to checking in on us we were totally back in our respective seats – side by side. "So, two little 'b's means blue eyes," Rob adlibbed – reading off my biology notebook which was open in front of us.

"What happened to Trig?" my mother asked.

"Oh, Rob's just helping me with Bio," I said casually

"Well, that's nice..." my mother said sounding mildly suspicious. "But you're not getting paid to be tutored; you're getting paid to tutor."

"Oh, yeah, of course Mrs. Morgan," Rob answered for me. "Mia's doing a great job, we're just taking a break."

"To study genetics?"

By the way she said it, I thought for a moment she suspected something. She glanced at the table where our phones were sitting within easy reach. She raised an eyebrow. "Do I need to take your phones away?"

I smiled sheepishly. "No, we're good. Going back to math right now."

She nodded and let the dining room door swing closed behind her.

"That was close," I said, but Rob was looking at my homework.

"Look," he said, pointing to the page. "It's you."

"Huh?"

"You know big B and little b? That's you – get it?" He looked at my boobs and raising his eyebrows comically.

"Hilarious," I said.

"Sexy," he corrected.

CHAPTER 19

Rollercoasters

Mid November

After that, Rob took to calling me Little b and, okay, as corny as it was, I loved it. It was so private and intimate that whenever he said it, I felt secret and special and like Rob Starr was really, actually mine.

But the feeling never lasted very long. Even though Rob and I were happy whenever we were alone, at school things were weirder than ever. Whenever I saw him, he was surrounded by his basketball buddies and a Baditude or three. He always said hello when he saw me, in an annoyingly convincing, just-friends way. And if he stopped to talk for even a minute, his actual friends grew impatient, bouncing the ever-present basketball loudly while they waited.

When they walked away, I was left feeling betrayed and jealous. Rob and Chloe's relationship had been so public, so romantic. Whenever Rob and I kissed, we were alone. Not that I wanted an audience or anything but there must have been something nice about not caring who saw how much you liked each other. Instead our relationship was confined to my dining room. I would "help Rob with Trig" every Tuesday and Thursday after school which

became our code for fooling around. We did attempt to study sometimes, for tests and quizzes and stuff and Rob was doing better –
good enough to keep him on the team – which was the goal. But the
majority of the time we spent either flirting or macking or well…
more than macking. In fact, things were getting the point that we
were going to require more privacy than the dining room if we
were going to go any further.

And now that we're on the subject, I should admit that, for
me at least, it seemed as if everything was moving very fast.
Don't get me wrong, it was nice… great even, but it was also
confusing. For one thing, I didn't really know how fast things
were supposed to go. Or in what order things should happen.
And, when and if we got around to doing some of those things,
exactly how was I supposed to know how to do them if I'd never
done them before?

And then there was the terrifying prospect of getting naked.
The idea of being naked in front of Rob completely freaked me out.
I mean, have you seen the girls on the internet? How was I going to
compete with that? And let's not forget, the flawless Chloe Olsen.
After her, how would he ever be happy with my doughy thighs or
the zits I sometimes got on my back?

In Rob's defense, he never really said anything or did anything to make me feel "less than". In fact, the opposite was true.
He complimented me a lot, especially when we were fooling
around. He would get this sort of puppy dog look on his face
and he'd tell me how beautiful I was and all that kind of stuff.
He even told me he loved me, and not just when we were fooling
around.

So now you're probably wondering why I didn't share this
critical piece of information as soon as he said it the first time.
The answer is, because couldn't remember the actual first time. I

think it might have been one night after we got back from visiting
his mom. It was late, and I was coming out of the bathroom after
brushing my teeth and he was waiting to go in and we were alone
in the dark hallway and he leaned over and gave me a really quick
kiss and said, "Goodnight. Love you."

He said it so casually and naturally that I wondered if he'd
even realized he said it. Maybe he'd said it by mistake. Or maybe
he'd said it before in a more significant way and I had somehow
missed it. But after that, he said it all the time. He would even write
b143 in my notebooks on pages I hadn't turned to yet so when I
got there, I would find the secret message. The lower-case b was
me (of course) and if you don't know, 143 is code for I (one letter)
love (four letters) you (three letters). At first, I'd thought he made
up this little code because of the Trig thing; like we wouldn't have
been together if it wasn't for math or something. I know… I'm a
cheeseball. Eventually though, I discovered that he hadn't invented
it at all. In fact, zillions of people use 143 to convey their affection.
But that didn't matter to me. It didn't make it any less romantic
when I opened a fresh page in my notebook and found his messy
handwriting there.

So, I was in love with Rob (of course) and he, incomprehen-
sibly, was in love with me. And it felt, to me at least, the way
all the songs said it would. One day I would be goofy-stupid,
Christmas-morning-when-you're-six-years-old kind of happy
and the next, desperately, painfully, country-music kind of sad.
But most of the time I was somewhere in between. Caught on a
thrilling, terrifying roller coaster ride; holding on so tight I could
barely breathe.

Besides our study sessions, the only other time Rob and I
got to be together was when we visited his mom every Monday,
Wednesday, and Saturday for two hours each time.

I know it sounds like it must have been awful, but it wasn't. I admit it was weird going to the rehab center, especially at first, but it was sort of interesting too. Mrs. G-S was steadily, but very slowly, improving. She still couldn't talk very well, or walk, or use her hands much. The therapist gave us all sorts of exercises to do with her that were supposed to help this kind of thing. We showed her different familiar objects to see if she could identify them. We moved around the room and spoke to see if she could respond to the change of location. Sometimes we let her touch different textures or played music or had her try to pick up brightly colored plastic toys. In a lot of ways, it was like teaching a baby. Looking back on this now, I can't imagine how weird this must have been for Rob or Jake who often came with us – seeing their mother so helpless and having to take care of her, not knowing if she'd ever be the person they knew; the person who'd always taken care of them. It must have been terrifying.

In all honesty, I didn't truly register the intensity of the situation. I went because Rob wanted me to, and it was more time I got to be with him. Don't get me wrong – I knew it was a big deal and all, it was just that I never really worried that much about Mrs. G-S. Somehow, I think I always knew she was going to recover. Perhaps it was because every so often I'd catch her looking at me with a knowing look in her eyes. Out of all the adults, I think she was the only one who figured out about me and Rob, which was amazing, considering.

I also liked the fact that I was the person Rob could talk to about all this stuff. From what I could tell, his friends didn't care all that much. But Rob and I talked about his mom all the time: how she was doing, what the doctors were saying, if we'd heard (or overheard) anything from my parents or Rob's dad.

I ended up having to give up band to do all this stuff, but my parents were okay about it. In fact, my mom was so proud that I was participating in Mrs. Gerber-Starr's recovery that she teared-up every time she dropped us off at the rehab center where Mrs. G-S now lived.

So, I guess what I'm saying is, that Rob and I were dealing with some serious stuff – stuff that was way beyond just me and Rob liking each other or hooking up. And that's why I thought it was really different with me and him, why it felt so real.

Ellsworth High School Case #1141
Transcript of interview: March 22
Student: Mia Morgan
Counselor: Dr. Janis Dubrovski

Dr. Dubrovski: *You can't think of a single thing that might have happened this year that might have prompted this event?*

Mia Morgan: *Not really, no.*

Dr. Dubrovski: *Well, something has clearly changed for you, Mia. Up until just a few months ago you got straight A's. You kept your head down. Then, all of a sudden, you dropped out of both band and Art club. Your grades started to slip. I can't help but wonder if it's all related? You've never been...what I mean is... well, you've always... kept a low profile.*

Mia Morgan: *So?*

Dr. Dubrovski: *So, tell me what's been going on. Why have you been acting and well...dressing so differently?*

CHAPTER 20

The Baditudes

Late November

I was suddenly really busy. Even without band practice, I had Rob's mom, Rob's tutoring, plus my own schoolwork to do (although in all honesty, grades were hardly my top priority anymore). And I had started spending quite a bit of time with the Baditudes. Yes, go ahead and reread the last sentence because it's a weird one for sure. But it was true. Ever since Rob had claimed me as his "friend" they had kind of adopted me. Maybe it was a way of thanking me (and my family) for taking care of him while his mom was sick. I don't know. There certainly wasn't any other reason for them to like me, and I certainly wasn't about to ask.

But before I get into the whole Baditude thing, let me just say, in my own defense, that I had no friends. Seriously – I'm not trying to be dramatic here. Ever since the bonfire, not a single person in my friend group – girl or boy – had spoken to me. And yeah, I got it, I was a jerk for walking away from them at the bonfire – I was an asshole for breaking our stupid seventh grade pact, or maybe they thought I should have tried to include them somehow or shouldn't have gone with Rob at all but... whatever. Was it really that bad? Bad enough that you would just stop talking to someone for forever?

The only person willing to hang out with me was Sally Verma. Sometimes we walked to school together, and sometimes she let me sit with her at lunch; but you couldn't really count her as an actual friend because we didn't actually like each other. The only reason she hung out with me was because I knew Rob, and because she barely had any friends of her own.

And I know it's low; to hang out with people you don't really like because you're desperate. But please don't judge me on this one. I don't know about your high school, but mine is not a place you want to face on your own.

I didn't even have my team or club friends to fall back on. Track had ended for the season, and I'd gotten kicked out of Art club for missing so many meetings. So, when the Baditudes started being nice to me and asking me to do stuff, I was just so grateful. No, it was more than that. I was flattered, honored, privileged. I mean, imagine if you had no friends and then the coolest, most popular kids in the school started asking you to hang out with them. You wouldn't be sitting around contemplating if you should go or not. Saying 'no' wasn't even an option.

As you might imagine, it was beyond weird at first; almost – if not actually weirder – than secretly dating Rob Starr. And I was totally uncomfortable pretty much the entire time.

There were about a dozen Baditudes in all, and at the center of the group were four girls Casey O'Hare, Kendal Carver, Candie Anderson and of course Chloe Olsen. I'm not sure if it was a requirement that all their names started with the "k" sound or just a kute koincidence. And while they had this in common, the most surprising thing I can tell you about them is that they were all so different. I guess that seems obvious – people are different – but from the outside, where I had been up to that point, it had always seemed like they were exactly the same.

Take Candie Anderson for instance. While most of the Baditudes were passable students, Candie was an honor student, on the debate team and had a 4.1 GPA – all while being vice-captain of the cheer squad. She was one of those all-around perfect kids your parents secretly (or maybe not so secretly) wish you would be. She was pretty too. Her dark skin was flawless, and her hair was perfectly arranged in long, uniform braided rows. She didn't smile or talk much –. But, her quietness, only made her appear stronger and more mature than the others – which it turns out, she wasn't.

Then there were Casey and Kendal who'd been best friends since the third grade. Until I started to hang out with them, I truly had trouble telling them apart. But in reality, they were practically opposites.

While they both had long, blond hair (real-ish for Casey, not so real for Kendal), amazing bodies and pretty faces, that was where the similarity ended. Kendal had hard features and her skin was sort of rough looking as if she'd spent too much time in the sun. Casey's face was of the softer, rounder variety. She was friendly and simple. And when she smiled her eyes nearly disappeared behind her full cheeks.

Casey talked a lot, mostly about stupid stuff like getting new uniforms or how hard it was to find the right hairspray to keep her recently cut side bangs out of her eyes when she cheered. She spent most of her time either working out or macking with her equally boring boyfriend, Luke Greenburg. Luke was a defensive lineman on the football team. Everyone called "Iceburg" because he was so big and hard to move.

Kendal, like her cheekbones, was sharper and more aggressive than Casey. In fact, I'm pretty sure it was she who threw the beer at me at the bonfire (but I wasn't about to ask for confirmation on that one). She didn't have a boyfriend and didn't seem to want one. She'd hooked up with most of the popular guys (Rob excluded, of course) and supposedly gave blow jobs to any guy on the basketball team that wanted one.

I'm guessing some of you are probably a little horrified right now – or maybe not – but I know I was. I mean, I'd heard about Kendal, everyone had, but I'd just assumed it was one of those jealous rumors people make up about popular girls to make themselves feel better about not being popular. In Kendal's case, however, it was all true. Or at least according to her it was. And she talked about it all the time. She'd compare the guys – who was "big" and who wasn't – and what sort of face they made when they came. I'm not kidding. Sometimes she'd even make the noises. She thought it was hilarious.

Okay, so maybe I sound like a total prude here, but this was just WAY beyond what I'd talked about with any of my friends – ever. I mean, I'd never given anyone a blow job (surprise, surprise). But even so, I could imagine what it was like. And while I wasn't marching against the idea or anything, I was pretty sure I didn't want to do it to every guy I met. I did my best to pretend that I thought it was all perfectly normal, but Kendal was on to me. She sensed how freaked out I was. I think she got even more graphic just to watch me squirm.

And then, of course, there was Chloe.

CHAPTER 21

Chloe

Late November

It was Chloe who first invited me to sit with the Baditudes at lunch. And it was Chloe who went on about how nice me and my family were to help Rob and Jake and their little sister while Mrs. G-S was in the hospital. And Chloe who encouraged me to talk and laughed at my jokes, and Chloe who pointed out my good qualities to the others. She'd say things like "Doesn't Mia (pronounced correctly) have the best calves? And she doesn't even work out!" Or "Mia says, like, the funniest stuff." Or "Mia listens to all these new bands I've, like, never even heard of." And okay, sure, even then I noticed that her compliments, if you really listened to them, could also sort of be insults, as in: Mia's out of shape, Mia says strange things, and Mia has weird taste in music. It was confusing. Especially when, every once in a while, she'd say something that sounded genuinely nice. Like once, when we were sharing a mirror in the girl's bathroom she said, "You really are pretty Mia. It's seems, like, crazy that nobody, like, noticed before," (she said "like" a lot). And despite all I knew about her and everything I'd heard, I, like, totally fell for it.

One afternoon, the Baditudes, took me to the mall and spent more than two hours helping me pick out new clothes, stuff I would have never considered myself. Short skirts and miniature, impractical tops. Chloe even convinced me to buy this bright coral, padded push-up bra. Not that it took much convincing – I mean, once you've tried one on and seen the difference (significant in my case). Let's just say, they basically sell themselves.

Looking back on this I realize that this gesture of "kindness" was as much for them as it was for me. Looking good was their currency and they couldn't exactly hang out with somebody as completely un-Baditude as I was. And while I knew I'd been invited into the group based solely on my status as Rob's friend, I think they all sort of enjoyed the challenge of transforming me, and I was their very willing student. They gave me advice on how to deal with my hair (flat iron), my clothes (all new), the zit in the corner of my nose (products), my teeth (more products), my thighs (exercises), my fingernails (Nailed It on Sixth Street). Even my laugh needed a makeover because, according to Kendal, it sounded like the bark of a small, nervous dog. It was something I'd never noticed about myself and I was mortified. I mean, seriously, how did my parents and friends let me walk around with yellow teeth laughing like a Pomeranian for almost sixteen years?

But it wasn't just Chloe's fashion guidance or even her sage advice about sex (I'll get back to this) that made me start to trust her. It was her thumb – the one on her right hand. And yes, I know that sounds weird, but you see Chloe was just about as perfect as you could be – perfect skin, perfect hair, perfect teeth, perfect eyebrows (she claimed she didn't even have to pluck) perfect boobs (as previously discussed), perfect earlobes for a triple pierce…you get the idea. Everything was perfect – everything except for the cuticle on her right thumb. It was chewed and red and really kind of gross. I even caught her gnawing at it a couple of times – once when she was driving us to The Skinny Salad and another time when she was studying for Chemistry in the library. And I suppose because I wanted to, I believed that her ripped-up cuticle told a deeper story. It said Chloe Olsen – perfect Chloe Olsen – wasn't really perfect after all. She was human and stressed, and maybe even a little scared just like the rest of us. It made me like her more than any compliment ever could.

On top of all that, and to her credit, she never asked me about Rob. Not once. And she knew how much time he and I spent together. She knew about the Trig tutoring sessions, the recovery center visits, she even saw me hanging out with him at parties (I'll get back to that too). And let's not forget, he lived in my house. But she never said a word. Never asked me about the night at the bonfire or if anything had ever happened between us.

But let's go back to the conversation about sex. From what I could tell, every one of the Baditudes had or was having sex in some form or another – most of the time with their boyfriends but sometimes even just hooking up with the jocks and popular guys. And there was a always a lot of drama around it – who they were "talking" to or sexting with, or cheating on or being cheated on by. The only Baditude who seemed to stay above it all was Chloe. And while she was supposedly "talking to" the rich and gorgeous Reynolds Prince, she rarely, if ever, talked *about* him, which is why it was so shocking when she brought him up one day on the way home from cheer practice (and yeah, I know it's lame to go to someone's cheer practice but after all, I was me and they were them, and when Chloe Olsen says "wait for me so we can, like, walk home together," you just sort of do it).

So, there we were walking home – Chloe, Kendal, and me – and Chloe started complaining about how Reynolds was pressuring her to have sex with him. "That's always how it is with guys," she said meaningfully. "Once they've had sex, it's hard for them to go back to *not* having sex, you know?"

"Totally," (this from Kendal, nodding in knowing agreement).

"And it's not like we're little kids anymore," Chloe said. She paused and looked at me. "But I'm just not that into him. I mean if I was *in love* with him it would be, like, totally different."

My brain instantly started spinning. Why was she looking at me? Was I crazy or was Chloe trying to tell me something? But if so, what? Did she suspect I was in love with Rob? And if so, why on earth would she be encouraging me to have sex with him – because that's what it sort of sounded like to me. And let's be real, she must have assumed something was going on (or had gone on) given the whole bonfire thing, right? And if I was right, how could Rob and I having sex possibly benefit her? Especially since I was sure (totally and completely certain) she still liked him.

Here's how I knew: 1) She never flirted with him or talked to him or even went near him if she could help it, which would appear to most people that she wasn't interested in him. However, if you thought about it (as I had – at ORD levels) you'd realize it's just not normal. I mean when you're really friends with someone – *just* friends with them – you're relaxed around them – right? You goof around with them, you talk, you laugh, you even flirt a little because really there's no harm in it if you're really *just* friends. But Chloe ignored Rob, deliberately and intentionally – which meant something else entirely. 2) When Rob was around – ignore him as she might – her whole demeanor changed. Her body went on high alert – like a dog who's just heard a high-pitched whistle. And 3) Whenever all three of us were in the same room, I swear I could sense her watching Rob and me out of the corner of her eye, constantly calculating the distance between us.

So, if she suspected there was something going on between me and Rob (which she did), and she still liked him (which she did), it would seem like me and Rob having sex would be the last thing she would want. Right?

But I was way out of my league here. While all these thoughts circled around in my brain, there was something much more powerful going on. Chloe Olsen was sharing a confidence with me – letting me in on a secret – and maybe giving me some advice about boys in general (because really, how could she know anything about me and Rob?) And, I wondered, maybe she was right. Maybe Rob was becoming impatient with me or that he thought I was acting like a little kid whenever I stepped on the brakes.

But I'm getting ahead of myself here. The important thing was that I had somehow found a way to ignore all my instincts and to let myself believe that Chloe and I were becoming actual friends. And sure, part of it was the thumb thing and the push-up bra perhaps, but really, mostly I believed it because I wanted to, with all of my desperately uncool and uninitiated heart.

Surprisingly, I was also becoming friendly with Kendal. She and I lived only a couple of streets apart. So, since I was spending a lot of time with the Baditudes, we were often left to walk the last few blocks with only each other for company. In those private minutes, Kendal would confide in me about the other Baditudes and Chloe in particular. In fact, she talked about Chloe incessantly.

Once she told me that Chloe has a tutor "for everything" because she just "isn't that smart". Once she called her a "controlling bitch." Another time she revealed that she and Chloe had kissed each other "more than once". "It only happens when she's drunk," Kendal said, "but I think she's bi and doesn't want to admit it because she was too worried about what other people would think."

Of course, I couldn't help but wonder if that meant Kendal was also bi, but I wasn't sure it was cool to ask someone that, so I just kept quiet. Kendal said that Candie "hated" Chloe for hooking up with Reynolds (whom Candie had been hooking up with on and off for some time), but that Candie couldn't say anything or Chloe would turn everyone against her. "That's the thing with Chloe," Kendal claimed, "she does whatever she wants because everyone's afraid of her. Even the guys. They go out with her, even though they know she's just a big tease and never really does anything... except with Rob... of course."

I was shocked by the things she shared. It was serious, friendship-ending kind of stuff. So...why was she telling me? Yet here again, I just completely ignored my instincts. I decided that Kendal must just really need to confide in someone. And, the truth was, I liked hearing it.

In other words, their mean-girl magic worked like a charm on me. I was alternatively exhilarated and stressed out by their attentions and confidences, constantly insecure yet in some ways more self-assured than I'd ever been before. Just walking down the hall with them or sitting at their lunch table was a high – and the envy in everyone else's eyes was the drug. I found myself seeking it out – scanning the room for affirmation of my new status. And, whenever I glimpsed the raw longing in another girl's face, I swallowed the smug thrill like a spoonful of fat-free frozen yogurt. Okay, maybe I wasn't a full-on Baditude, but I'd become a sort of Baditude-in-training – dressing and acting like the very girls I'd criticized in the past and making fun of the girls who'd once been my friends.

And speaking of them, one afternoon we – the Baditudes and I – ran into them at the pizzeria. They were walking out when we arrived.

"Hi, Mia," Carmen said as we passed. My heart jumped. Were they speaking to me again? I was just about to reply when Kendal pushed up next to me and linked her arm in mine.

When we had walked a few steps past Carmen, Kendal turned and said (loud enough for Carmen to hear her) "Ew, who was that? And what made her think she could talk us?"

I glanced back at Carmen. Her face had turned bright red. All the Baditudes laughed – and I did too. I had no choice. At least that's what I wanted to believe.

If you're thinking 'wow, what an asshole' right now, you'd be dead right. Because not only was I turning my back on my actual friends, I was allowing myself to believe something I knew in my heart was a lie. The truth was right there in front of me the whole time had I asked myself one simple question: "Why?" Why were the Baditudes really hanging out with me? Why was Chloe being nice to me? I didn't have anything to offer them besides being "friends" with Rob, which was something they already had.

CHAPTER 22

Thanksgiving, Christmas & Basketball

November/ December

First things first: basketball. The team was off to a slow start. They'd lost the first two games, and Rob, who was both the captain and the star player, was understandably freaked out. He was realizing that even 'Rock Starr' at his best wasn't enough to make up for the fact that much of the last year's championship team had graduated in the Spring. On top of that pressure was the fact that this was Rob's his last chance to impress college recruiters. It wasn't that he needed scholarship money. He didn't. But it turns out Trig wasn't the only class he was struggling in and if he wanted to get into a good school, basketball was his ticket.

Rob was superstitious when it came to basketball, which meant that even though we weren't publicly a couple, he insisted I try to attend every game (you may recall the whole "good luck charm" thing when his mother came out of the coma?). And while this request was flattering and made me feel very important, it also made my life very complicated.

Going to the home games was easy enough, but the away games were much tougher to swing. I didn't have my driver's license yet and the cheerleaders all travelled by bus. This left two unsavory options: try to grab a ride with Sally Verma and Veronica or buddy up to Jake and see if one of his idiot friends would drive me. The whole thing was awkward and irritating, but whatever – I needed to be at those games.

To make matters worse, despite all my efforts to get to the games, I didn't get to spend any time with Rob. In fact, the only interaction we had occurred when Rob was on the free-throw line. He'd bounce the ball twice, then pause and look up in the stands. He tried to be casual, like he wasn't looking for anyone in particular, but he'd always find me. Then, when our eyes met, I would give him a private, almost imperceptible nod. He'd bounce the ball one more time and make the shot. It wasn't much, but it almost made the trouble of getting there worthwhile. He almost never missed.

● ● ●

On Thanksgiving, the Morgans and the Starrs (minus Bill, who was away on business) spent the afternoon at the rehab center and it was – as you can imagine – totally horrible. They had those paper turkeys on all the tables – you know the kind with the globe of orange, honeycomb tissue paper in the middle. Mrs. Gerber-Starr was propped up in a wheelchair with my mother's homemade dinner on a tray in front of her. Her hair had been freshly washed and cut, but instead of looking better it made her look less familiar – her signature blond all but gone and what was left, a sort of blah, gray-brown. My mother had attempted to do her makeup – for the pictures – but it only made things worse. The cheerful pink lipstick was practically dayglo in the harsh, antiseptic light of the cafeteria. Rob said nothing the whole afternoon.

As soon as we finished eating, Rob excused himself, saying he needed some air. When he didn't come back, Jake and I went outside to look for him. We found him in the back parking lot throwing rocks into the woods behind the facility. Even at a distance you could see the tension in his body. Rob ignored us until Jake called to him, "Hey, everyone's waiting in the car." Rob threw one more rock and it hit a tree with a loud smacking sound. When we got back to the house, Reynolds was parked at the curb waiting for him. I'm not sure where he went but he didn't come back until much later that night.

December was a messy blur of activity; basketball games, shopping and exams (my lowest scores ever) more games, waiting for Rob to get home from practice, waiting for Rob to get home after games, and the few treasured "Trig sessions" where we could be alone together.

Rob was so busy with the team he didn't have much time for rehab center visits. Of course, I still went. I couldn't *not* go just because he wasn't there. If I did, it would look like I had only been going to be with Rob, which was only sort of true. I was honestly kind of interested in all the medical stuff. It was cool to see the therapy working. Jake came with me most of the time and was actually pretty nice to hang out with – on his best behavior in front of is mom, I guess.

One time, when Mrs. G-S had fallen asleep, Jake admitted to me how scared he was. He was worried his mother might never be herself again. He said that the idea of having a confused and helpless mother was, in some ways, scarier than the idea of losing her altogether. All I could think was, poor Rob. He must be feeling the same way. No wonder he avoided the visits.

When Rob did come with me, he was often in a bad mood, especially if the team had lost their recent game, so I did everything I could think of to keep things positive for him. I made sure to point out all Mrs. G-S's improvements and remind him how all the doctors told us it could take a long time. But the reality was, nobody really knew what was going to happen to Mrs. G-S and nothing I could say would change that fact.

And then it was Christmas (and Hanukah) and with them came the whirl of Ellsworth parties, food, Secret Santa gift swaps and more visits to the rehab center.

Rob and Jake moved home temporarily to make room for my grandparents to stay a few days and I was almost instantly miserable. I hadn't realized how much I counted on seeing Rob at dinner or watching TV or in the mornings.

On Christmas Eve, the Starrs came over and Rob and I snuck into my room to exchange presents. Rob gave me a small stuffed bear holding a heart that said LOVE on it and one of his old basketball sweatshirts. It wasn't the one he wore all the time because well, he still wore that one all the time, but another one that he found in his room when he moved back home for that week between Hanukah and Christmas.

In case you're wondering, I gave Rob a stocking full of stuff; basketball socks, some chocolate chip cookies that I made with both dark and milk chocolate chips. I also got him a vape pen to replace one he'd lost in the Derby High School parking lot after a game. As you can imagine it was pretty hard to get a pen in Ellsworth when you're underage, but luckily Sally's friend Veronica had a fake i.d.

And the answer to your next questions is yes. Yes, I did notice that I had put more effort (and money) into the whole Christmas / Hanukah thing than Rob had. And at first, I really didn't care. Rob gave me things that meant something. Not like the stuff the Baditudes got from their silly boyfriends – tickets to a concert,

Chanel perfume, white gold hoops. And they posted so many pictures it was obvious they were showing off.

But then Casey posted a pic of her gift from Ice. He got her that Tiffany necklace – you know, the one with the silver heart that hangs sideways from the chain? And honestly, I really wouldn't have cared, except that I was with Chloe and Kendal when the post popped up. When Chloe saw it, she rolled her eyes and said, "Can you believe Casey and that stupid Tiffany necklace? I mean, Rob gave me the exact same necklace like, two years ago. Get over yourself!"

So, as I was saying, I loved the stuff Rob got me. At least it was personal and romantic (even if I could never wear the sweatshirt anywhere) and way better than some stupid necklace that every third girl on earth (or at least in Ellsworth) got for her sweet sixteen. But once I knew that somewhere in the pile of trinkets in Chloe's jewelry box was a little, silver, Tiffany heart, picked out and paid for by Rob Starr, I was tortured. Why had Rob spent so much money on Chloe? Did he care about her more than me or was it just because he knew everyone would see what he got her, but no one would ever know what he got me? Either way, it sucked.

CHAPTER 23

Barty Time

End of December

By the last week in December Mrs. Gerber-Starr's doctors declared that her slow but steady improvement meant she had a good chance of making a full recovery. This news, good as it was, brought trouble for me. It meant that my mother, who had spent the last many weeks focusing on Madeline, could now resume her normal level of focus on me. And while she definitely hadn't figured out that Rob and I were together (thank God), she did finally notice that something was going on. Like, why weren't my friends walking with me to school anymore? And more concerningly, what's with my new clothes?

You see, over the past several weeks, I'd used the money I'd earned tutoring Rob to buy myself a Baditude-approved wardrobe. I was going for a sort of hot-preppy look with a lot of leg because Chloe informed me that my legs were *by far* my best quality (and in saying so clearly inferred that my butt, boobs and face weren't even in the running).

Just a note on that – isn't it weird how we judge ourselves (and each other) in parts rather than as a whole? Like, I don't know how many times I wished I had nicer boobs or better hair or thinner thighs. It must be because that's how guys talk about us; compartmentalizing us into legs or breasts as if they're shopping for a barbeque. Sure, I know the hot guys from the not so hot, but I honestly couldn't tell you which five guys in my high school had the best butts. Well, maybe, if I thought about it....

Anyway, regardless of how backhanded Chloe's compliment was, I took her advice to heart. My go-to outfit was a short (*very* short) pleated mini in black, grey, navy or plaid, with a loose sweater and boots. I wore my hair straight every day which took a lot of time but was worth it because Rob (and pretty much every other boy I encountered) seemed to like it better that way. I still kept my makeup simple but had gotten a little heavy handed with the mascara, which my mother pointed out one morning on the way to school.

"I'm just trying something new," I explained. But Calista wasn't so easily put off. She started asking a lot of questions. Where did I get all the new clothes? Did I want to talk? Was there someone I was "interested in" at school?

I'm not sure exactly when I'd turned into someone else, but there, in that moment, while my mother barraged me with questions, I knew that I had. It was as if it had been years (rather than weeks) since I'd hung out with Carmen or Stephanie watching old Star Wars movies – as if last summer's Math Camp was as much a part of my past as the American Girl dolls in the plastic bin in the basement.

Instead of answering my mother's questions, I resorted to the classic teenage deflection methods I'd seen other kids use on their parents: "Can't a person just try to look nice for school without getting the third degree? *God!*"

I'd never spoken that way to my mom before, and I think we

were both kind of surprised how effective it was. My mother, Command Central Calista, backed off. I think she said something like, "Of course Mia, that's not what I'm saying. I'm just wondering why now? But if you want to try and look...nicer for school, that's fine." I wasn't sure if she just didn't know how to deal with me or if she just chose to let it go. Either way, the New Mia didn't care. I got what I wanted, which was for her to leave me alone.

However, my parents had yet to see my second quarter grades. I'd made it through first quarter with okay scores – just slightly lower than usual and it was easy enough to attribute that to the Mrs. G-S stuff. Now, however, I was down to an eighty-six average. It was the first time I'd ever been below an A in well...ever. And I wasn't sure how long I could blame it on Mrs. Gerber-Starr, even if she was legitimately part of the problem.

Of course, the real problem was Rob. I thought about him all the time. I was distracted by him even when we weren't together. And, as hard as I tried to concentrate on other things, I couldn't seem stop myself.

I wish I could tell you I was consumed with worry about his mom or his grades or whether the basketball team was going to make it to the finals or even that I was fantasizing about kissing him but...no. What occupied my brain were classic Obsessive Repulsive Disorder thoughts: What is he doing right now? Are there girls there? Is Chloe there? Samantha Hernandez? Does he like Samantha? Does he still like Chloe? Did I see them look at each other in the lunch room the other day or was it just me being paranoid? Why did he like that pic of Casey in a bikini over Christmas break? Did he think Casey was prettier than me? She does have way bigger boobs. Does he think my boobs are too small? Is it okay that he is liking other girl's pictures when I'm supposed to be his girlfriend? Do other girls let their boyfriends like pictures of girls in bikinis? Did he do that stuff when he was with Chloe?

I kept telling myself that what I was feeling and thinking was normal – that it was just a symptom of the situation we were in; that if Rob and I didn't have to hide our relationship from everyone, I wouldn't be so concerned. But some part of me knew that wasn't true. Somewhere, buried deep, I understood that how I was feeling wasn't right – that no one should feel sick-to-your-stomach worried about their relationship all the time.

Sadly, I wasn't ready to face that truth yet – so I pushed it down deeper and pretended I was fine. But the closer Rob and I got, the more terrified I became of losing him.

To make matters even more difficult, one night, sort of out of the blue, Rob invited me to one of the Baditude parties or barites as they called them – which were (of course) the most exclusive parties in Ellsworth. He said that Casey told him to invite me – it was at her house – and that she had forgotten to mention it to me after school because she had practice. As you can imagine, I was psyched. I mean I couldn't believe I was invited to a real high school party, let alone a barty. On top of that, I was FINALLY going to hang out with Rob in public like it was a perfectly normal thing to do. Sure, we were going to have to act like we were just friends, but so what? Anything was better than sitting at home wondering what he was doing.

It wasn't going to be easy though. Me going to a party of any kind was complicated. I wasn't allowed to go anywhere without telling my parents all the details. Would the parents be home? Was there going to be alcohol there? Plus, since my mother knew just about everyone in town, there was always the chance that she might decide to call the house – and you can imagine the horror of that possibility.

So, I didn't go.

Ha! Just kidding. Of course, I went. I did what every high school student does when they want to go someplace they're not supposed to be: I lied. I said I had a study group at the library. And that was that. I'm embarrassed to say how easy it was. I lied, and my parents believed me. Why wouldn't they? I'd never given them a reason not to. Still, given the change in my outward appearance, you'd think they'd have asked a few more questions. But they didn't. They never doubted me.

The plan was that Rob and I would leave the house separately so my parents would not suspect anything. He'd go to the barty, (I'm just going to use the word party from now on because barty is just completely obnoxious) about twenty minutes before me. Then I would head out to the "library".

Rob's friends picked him up as planned. And I waited at home, trying to solve the classic girl-dilemma of finding something both warm *and* cute to wear. I settled on some tight jeans and a cropped, shoulder-baring sweater. Then, at the allotted time, I headed out into the freezing night. It was snowing lightly, and the ground was covered in fluffy white powder.

When I reached Casey's street, I texted Rob. I wasn't exactly sure which house was hers, so, even if I had felt comfortable enough to just head into the party, I was sort of stuck waiting for him. It took him about ten or fifteen minutes to come out, and by that time I was totally frozen.

When I spotted him heading towards me from halfway down the block, I could tell he was already a little buzzed. I was gearing up to be annoyed, but when he reached me, he grabbed me and wrapped me in a giant hug, rubbing my back and arms to warm me up. He tucked my scarf more snugly around my neck and blew on my freezing fingers. The streetlight on the corner made a perfect circle of light on the newly fallen snow and we stood there, just outside that circle – like standing in the shadow of a snow globe – and we kissed, and the combination of warm kisses and cold January air was like a Hallmark movie come to life.

Then, Rob pulled away and said happily, "C'mon, it's freezing out here."

As we headed down the street, I hastily fixed my lip gloss and smoothed my hair, and generally tried to look like (and believe) that I belonged at a Baditude party. When we got to the door, Rob pushed it open as if it were his own house and stepped inside confidently. And that's where the good part of the evening ended. I squeezed in behind him and shrugged off my coat. A couple of Rob's friends greeted him as soon as we walked in and then he was off. It took less than a minute for us to get separated.

I stood alone for a minute, not knowing what to do. I finally decided to find the bathroom and fix myself up a little. When I found it, there was a line – of course. Kendal and Candie were waiting there. When they saw me, they were pleasant enough in a "Hey Mia" sort of way, but they were busy too gossiping about something to pay much attention to me.

About twenty minutes later, after I had finally gotten in and out of the bathroom, I found Rob in the kitchen. I positioned myself near him – but not next to him – and Mike Egan handed me a beer. He tried to talk to me for a minute or two, but I couldn't really hear him very well over the noise and music. I guess I said "what?" one too many times because when a Heam Tottie waved a vape pen in his face, he grinned and followed her out the side door of the kitchen without looking back.

Rob was only a few feet away from me, but he might as well

have been at a different party altogether. While I stood alone near the kitchen door, Rob leaned against the counter, the center of a large rolling crowd. The boys vied for his attention with jokes or drinks or anecdotes of one of Rob's epic basketball shots and girls buzzed around him like giggly moths. I stood just outside of the circle and sipped at my beer.

Occasionally Rob noticed me. Every once in a while, he winked at me or asked me if I'd grab him a beer from the fridge. But most of the time, he barely seemed to know I was there. As for the Baditudes, they were far to busy hosting or macking or drinking to pay any attention to me.

The only other person who spoke to me all night (besides Mike and occasionally Rob) was a good-looking hurdler named Carlos Chin who I sort of knew because he sat behind me in fourth period English. He came up to me and told me he was going to have to change seats in class because he couldn't concentrate with me sitting in front of him. "Shut up!" I said and pushed his shoulder flirtatiously. Not the wittiest comeback I'll admit but I'd picked up a few things from my new cheer friends and one of them was, most guys don't give a crap about wit unless it shows up in some cute cutoffs.

Surprisingly, Rob noticed him talking to me. He came over to me and threw a protective arm around my shoulders – which you would think I would be happy about except that it was all so casual and older-brotherish that it made me feel even worse. Carlos disappeared into the crowd. But Rob hung out there, with his arm around me, for a while. In case you were wondering, arms weigh about five percent of a person's total body weight which means that Rob's arm weighed about nine pounds – which is a lot have draped over your shoulder for like twenty minutes, even if it does make you feel like the prettiest kid sister in the room.

Chloe was there, of course, and if you think she didn't notice that Rob had is arm around me, you'd be dead wrong. She noticed everything that night. In fact, if I ever thought that maybe she was getting over him, I knew that night for sure that she wasn't. Sure, she barely spoke to Rob, but she wasn't fooling me. I saw how she watched him; how she carefully positioned herself in the room, holding court in a spot where she could see Rob (and he could see her) without being too obvious. Whenever she thought he might be listening, her conversations became more animated, her movements more pronounced, her laughter ringing at a higher, sharper pitch. "Stop it, Peter (or Mark or Reynolds...)" she'd say loudly, then her eyes would flicker over to Rob to gauge his reaction.

I had to keep reminding myself that I couldn't be mad at her. I was pretty sure she didn't know that Rob and I were together. I mean, she would never be friends with me if she thought we were. Still, it bugged me. Mostly because she was just so pretty and always had on the perfect, cute-girl outfit and was just generally about a thousand times more daz than I could ever be. Still, despite all her efforts and all her perfectness, Rob seemed remarkably oblivious – which I'm sure drove her crazy.

I left the party at ten-fifteen (I had a ten-thirty curfew) and walked home alone. It sucked. Not just because it was cold and snowy but because Rob stayed, a full hour and half longer than I did.

After that night, going to the Baditude parties became a sort of regular thing. I got used to going and people got used to me being there. But I never stopped wondering what went on in those ninety minutes between ten-thirty and midnight.

CHAPTER 24

Birthday Surprise

January 3rd

January third was Mrs. Gerber-Starr's birthday. It was also the day the first of three serious things happened. We – Rob, me, my mom, Mr. Starr, and Jake headed to the rehab center around mid-morning. Everyone was quiet on the way over, most notably Mr. Starr, who seemed irritated by something, though we hadn't seen him in a couple of weeks. When we arrived, we were met by one of Mrs. G-S's doctors who informed us that, while they continued to be optimistic about her recovery, the new medication they'd been trying didn't seem to be having much effect. And although no one said so, it didn't sound like great news.

While my mother engaged Mrs. G-S in her exercises, Mr. Starr paced impatiently. At one point his phone went off and he stepped out into the hall to take the call. When he came back, he was even more agitated then before. And just so you get the full picture, Mr. Starr wasn't really the type of guy to get frazzled. He was one of those men that wore a jacket everyday – even on the weekends – even in the summer. My father always joked that Bill could play three sets of tennis without breaking a sweat, so it was a little unsettling to see him so jumpy.

He put his phone in his pocket and announced he was going to have to cut the visit short. He insisted we sing Happy Birthday which was weird and sad because Mrs. G-S didn't really know what was going on. Plus, it turned out that the Starrs were all totally tone deaf – so all in, it was arguably one of the worst "Happy Birthday" renditions in history.

Then Mr. Starr sat on the edge of the bed and pulled a small gift box out of his jacket pocket. He placed it in Mrs. Gerber-Starrs' hands. When Mrs. G-S didn't respond – didn't even register that there was a gift – Mr. Starr began to plead with her.

"Come on Madeline. Please. Take the gift. Please..." He sighed loudly. "They're diamond earrings," he added, as if that would somehow make a difference.

So, I probably don't have to say this but, if I could have beamed myself out of there you can bet I would have – the whole scene was way too private and way too sad for all of us to be standing there watching. And it only got worse.

Mr. Starr tried again to get her to take the earrings – but she just vaguely looked down at the box and frowned. When he still got no reaction his voice suddenly changed, "For God's sake Madeline… you live for this shit." He snatched the box from her hands and threw it on the floor. I looked over at Rob, but he didn't notice. He was staring at his father, wide-eyed. Then I turned to Jake and he looked back at me. I expected him to look sad or scared but there was something else in his face.

My mother put her hand on Bill's shoulder. "I think we've all had enough for today," she said. "Mia and I will stay for a while. Why don't you take the boys and tell them the good news?" When Mr. Starr didn't say anything, my mother turned to Rob and Jake and said, "your father is going to move you back home tonight."

I think I must have gasped in surprise because my mother shot me a look that said, "This doesn't concern you, Mia."

But when my mother turned her attention back to Mr. Starr, he was looking at her intently – stress carving deep lines in his forehead.

"Or not..." she said slowly. "You know they can stay with me as long as you need them too, Bill. If it's too much with your work and all this," she gestured at the medical equipment next to Mrs. Gerber-Starr's bed, "then just leave them where they are. They're doing fine with us – they're just fine."

Mr. Starr shook his head, then nodded, then shook his head again. "I don't know how to thank you. I... I think it might be best. It's just with all the travelling and if it's not too..."

"Cut the shit, Dad," Jake said loudly, startling all of us. "Just stop," he almost shouted. His voice sounded tight and strangled. "You don't give a shit about any of this...about us. I know what's going on with you and that lady from your office. I went to our house the week after mom's accident to get my mouthguard. It wasn't even a week. It was like... five days... five days after the accident. And I heard you and her. I heard you..." he paused and swallowed hard. "So, all this shit about it being for the best..."

Mr. Starr stood up and walked quickly towards Jake as if he might hit him, but Jake didn't move. "Are you going to deny it?" Jake asked, standing his ground. He looked into his father's face accusingly and I realized they were almost the same height. I hadn't noticed how tall Jake had grown – he was at least as tall as Rob. "Well, are you?" Jake said. There was a slight tremor in his voice.

Mr. Starr smacked Jake in the mouth – right there in hospital room.

He must have hit him pretty hard because he knocked Jake off balance. Jake steadied himself and slowly put his hand to his face. His eyes welled with tears from the sting.

"What I do, young man, is my business," Mr. Starr said shaking his finger angrily.

"This isn't about fucking business," Jake shouted. "It's about mom." With that, Jake's voice broke. "You're such a selfish asshole," he snuffled through his tears.

"Okay let's everyone just calm down." My mother's face was pale, but her take-charge instinct was apparently shock-proof. "Bill, you should go home. Just take the car and go. I'll call a cab and the boys will come back to the house with me."

Mr. Starr began to speak but my mother spoke over him. "Just take the car and go," she said again. "I've got this. I've got them. It's fine."

Okay so here's what I was thinking:

1) Holy shit! That was totally scary.
2) Mr. Starr is a total asshole. But maybe I should have figured that out already since he basically dumped his kids at our house and was barely ever around.
3) The fact that Jake has been carrying this information around for a while really helped explain a lot of the douchiness.
4) Oh my God, did Mrs. Starr understand any of that?
5) I hope this doesn't mean that Rob and I aren't going to hook up tonight at Jenny Cardman's party. (And yes, I might be the most incredibly self-centered person on earth because that's honestly one of the things that went through my mind at that moment.)

6) But at least this probably means that Rob isn't moving out of our house, (and yes, I honestly thought this too.)

7) Except that it might be better if we didn't live in the same house anymore because maybe it's getting a little too familiar. I mean all we ever do as a couple is mess around in the dining room (and sometimes the upstairs bathroom) and go to parties where Rob hangs out with his friends while I stand next to him fake-laughing at his friends' stupid jokes.

Yes, it is embarrassing to admit all of my shallow, selfish, Rob-obsessed thoughts after the dramatic family scene I'd just witnessed. But I really couldn't help it. Rob was all I thought about anymore.

Ellsworth High School Case #1141
Transcript of interview: March 22
Student: Mia Morgan
Counselor: Dr. Janis Dubrovski

Dr. Dubrovski: *Some kids we've spoken to mentioned that you've attended several parties over the last few months. Is that true?*
Mia Morgan: *I guess.*
Dr. Dubrovski: *Okay. Well, maybe some of the kids at these parties are involved. Were you... hooking up with any of the boys at these events?*
Mia Morgan: *No. Nothing happened at those parties.*
Dr. Dubrovski: *What about the boys in the photographs. Had you had sex with either of the boys in the photographs before that night?*
Mia Morgan: *No. I didn't. And why would it matter? I mean, how would that change anything? It wouldn't make what they did okay.*
Dr. Dubrovski: *Of course not. That's not what I'm suggesting. I'm simply trying to understand the nature of your relationship with these kids.*
Mia Morgan: *I didn't have a relationship with either of those kids*
Dr. Dubrovski: *Okay...well...if you weren't with those kids, who were you with?*
Mia Morgan: *What do you mean?*
Dr. Dubrovski: *I mean, if you didn't come to the parties with them, who did you come with?*
Mia Morgan: *No one.*
Dr. Dubrovski: *You went to the parties alone?*

Mia Morgan: *Yes, I sort of...I knew people there. I was meeting people there.*

Dr. Dubrovski: *But you went by yourself...to the parties?*

Student: Mia Morgan: *Yeah. Is that a crime or something?*

Dr. Dubrovski: *It's unusual.*

CHAPTER 25

U Should Walk

January 3ʳᵈ continued

Rob did end up going to Jenny Cardman's party that night. I admit it was a little surprising given the fight between his dad and Jake earlier that day, but I figured he just needed to stop thinking for a while.

I didn't really know Jenny that well or even at all. She was a senior and she lived in a big house across town. Also, she was a HB&P and they were famously rich, snobby, girls – the kind that dress well, get good grades and go to small private colleges so they can meet boys from richer, snobbier towns than ours. But the only important part of what I just said was that she lived across town. And that was part of the second big thing that happened.

Ellsworth isn't a big town, so everyone's house is within walking distance. Still, Jenny's was a hike – like maybe twenty or twenty-five minutes. Rob left to go to the party around eight. One of his friends picked him up by car and Rob was supposed to text me as soon as he got there. Well, I didn't hear from him until around 8:53 and okay, it wasn't around 8:53 it was exactly 8:53 and

I know this because I'd been waiting to hear from him for forty-one minutes. Here's what the text said:

Rob: R u coming?

Me: Um, yeah. Can you get someone to pick me up at the corner?

Then nothing for like ten minutes

Rob: No luck. U should walk.

Walk? It was really cold out and it was late and dark and even though Ellsworth was a nice town and all, it isn't ever a great idea for a girl to walk around at night by herself – anywhere really.

Me: ok

I know I probably should have stayed home. There really wasn't any reason for me to go, except, as previously explained, I kind of hated it when Rob went to parties without me. I mean, I trusted him, but I hated thinking about all the girls trying to get his attention – Chloe in particular. And going was always a better option than sitting around ORDing and waiting for him to come home. Besides, it wasn't like I had anything else to do (except a paper in English and a chapter in Biology).

Then another... maybe, four minutes.

Rob: cool

That was it. So, I pulled on a huge Ellsworth sweatshirt and a jacket over the short denim skirt and tiny tank top I'd put on for the party, lied to my parents and headed out into the freezing night.

It took me twenty-four minutes to get there. When I arrived, there were a million cars and a bunch of seniors playing Frisbee on the front lawn even though – as I may have mentioned – it was really cold and really dark. Maybe they were just too drunk to care. I tried to walk past them without being noticed but one of the girls called out to me.

"Wrong house, kid."

"Uh… I'm meeting Rob here."

Now, just so you have the whole picture, at this point I've been out in the windy cold weather for almost a half hour in not enough clothing and I'd been walking faster than normal so I was sort of freezing and sweaty at the same time. I'm sure my nose was red, and it was definitely running, and my hair probably looked like straw.

"Who?"

"Rob Starr," I said, trying to sound confident – still moving toward the door.

She looked me over again. "Oh yeah…" she said with a tinge of laughter in her voice.

I just kept walking. I'd gotten used to that kind of reaction.

Once I was in the house – which was a million degrees and packed with kids I barely recognized – I made my way towards the kitchen, which took another six minutes or so, because there were so many people. I had to physically squeeze my way through them. But when I finally pushed my way into the kitchen, the only person I recognized was Justin who was even louder and more obnoxious than usual given that he was totally wasted. I angled my way through the crowd until I was standing near enough that he could hear me shout.

"Hey, have you seen Rob?"

"Hel-lo Mia. How 'bout a hug for your Uncle Justin?"

"Uh, I don't think so. I'm looking for Rob?"

"What do you need Rob for when I'm right here?"

"I just…do you know where he is?"

"Why are you always so boring?" Justin asked rolling his eyes.

I looked back at him blankly.

"He was just here," he said with a sigh. "Went out back to …"

Then he made the universal symbol for smoke a joint.

It took me another ten minutes before I found Rob. He was with a few other seniors on the back porch. It was now 9:47 which meant that in exactly nineteen minutes I had to leave if I wanted to make it home in time for my 10:30 curfew.

"Little beeee. Whaddya doing here, babe?" Rob talked all "dude" when he was high.

"Well, I, uh, just walked over to hang out." Did he forget he invited me?

"Holy shit. You walked all the way here?" At this point the conversation stopped and the three other guys were just looking at me and Rob.

"Uh, yeah. It's not that far," I mumbled. I was totally embarrassed. Rob didn't seem to notice.

"Aw, poor Little b. You must be freezing. C'mere." Rob grabbed my arm and pulled me down on his lap. He pushed his hands inside my many layers until his cold fingers found my skin. "Mmm, you don't feel cold."

I wanted to say, what the hell are you doing? Why are you acting like we're together in front of everyone? I didn't though. I just pulled away from him and said, "I'm guessing you've had a few beers?"

"Maybe a few…" he said laughing.

I laughed – but not really.

"Hey so, I, um, actually have to go. I'm going to be late."

One of the Seniors chuckled. And yes, I felt like a total ten-year-old. It was truly amazing the difference those few years between sophomore and senior could make.

"Shut up," Rob told them. Then to me, "Uh, sure, okay…" and it sounded, for a second, like he might be realizing he was being a jerk. But then he said, "I'll walk you out."

We pushed our way through the family room and we almost made it to the front hall before Rob was derailed by a bunch of guys near the pool table. I stood waiting awkwardly by the front door for several minutes. I finally left when I heard Rob's voice through the crowd. "I've gotta handle something, but then I'm coming back and I'm gonna teach you assholes the meaning of pool."

CHAPTER 26

Really?

January 3rd Late

By the time I got home, it was snowing pretty hard and I was frozen solid. "Hey, I'm home," I called to my parents as I walked in, then went straight upstairs. After quickly washing up, I went to my bedroom and locked the door. I was worried Rob would be home soon and I didn't want him trying to get in – not that he would – or at least he hadn't – at least not yet. And I lay awake for a long time – long enough to hear Rob come back – which, by the way, was two hours and eighteen minutes after I did. And I'm betting he didn't have to walk. Had he forgotten I was even there? I listened to him toss his house keys on the table at the bottom of the stairs and make his way upstairs. I'm not sure what time I fell asleep, but it was late enough that the light had already started to change outside my window.

Sunday was the day Rob and I always visited his mother at the rehab center. But I wasn't sure we were still going considering the events of the previous day and the previous night. I didn't know what to expect or how to feel. But that's not to say I didn't know *what* I felt. I felt angry. Really, genuinely angry. How could he have been so inconsiderate? BUT…shit. Shit, shit, shit. How was I supposed to be angry at Rob? He hadn't really done anything so terrible except get drunk and high and flake out a little. It wasn't like I walked in on him macking with some other girl or anything. And he'd had such a bad day and his father was such an asshole. And I knew that Rob didn't really handle stuff like that – you know, like stress, very well. He always got moody when the team lost, or his mother had a bad day, or he didn't do well on a test. So, maybe I should have figured he just wanted to hang with his friends. But if that was the case, why had he bothered to ask me to come?

I pulled on some old jeans and a sweatshirt. Since I hadn't slept much, I looked pretty bad, but honestly, I really didn't feel like trying to look good for Rob. He certainly didn't deserve it, but by now, it had become a habit. I wasn't that same girl that didn't wear makeup or put her hair in a ponytail without checking the mirror anymore. However, I wasn't going to kill myself either. I did as little as I felt I could get away with – some concealer under my eyes and on the little cluster of pimples that had formed on my forehead overnight – and mascara and lip balm, and a little blush because I was pale since I hadn't slept. Then a messy-cute ponytail which took several minutes but was worth it, so I didn't look like I was trying too hard. And no, at the time, I didn't realize how hard I was trying.

I could hear everyone in the kitchen and from the smell of things, my mother was making her famous waffles which really were totally delicious. It was her way of trying to heal the wounds of the day before. My father was talking as I walked in.

"… over in Green Ridge," he said.

"Wow," Rob replied sounding curious, "what happened?"

"Apparently, several cars were keyed on Washington Street," my father said turning the page of the paper to check his facts.

"I was at a party right near there; at the Cardman's house," Rob said, stuffing a huge forkful of waffles in his mouth.

"Did they catch whoever did it?" I asked.

My dad looked up from the paper. "Good-morning sweetheart," he said, "and no. They're asking if anyone knows anything to call it in."

"Hi honey," my mother said handing me a plate of waffles. "You'll have to squeeze in next to Robbie."

Rob dutifully started moving his plate over, then his chair.

"It's fine. I'll just sit over here at the counter."

"Oh, no honey, there's plenty of ..."

"Really mom, I'm fine right here." I popped a bite of waffle in my mouth. "Mmmm, great batch," I said to distract her.

"Really? Oh good. I wasn't sure the baking powder was fresh enough."

"They're perfect. Really." Which they were.

"Yes, Mrs. Morgan. They're awesome," Rob said in his basket-ball-boy-wonder voice. I felt a little like throwing my plate at him.

"Robbie, please – call me Calista. I mean, after all, you're going to be here another couple of weeks at least."

So, they weren't moving out. I felt a flood of relief wash over me.

"I'll make you a deal, Mrs. Morgan," he said, flashing his superstar smile, "I'll call you Calista if you *stop* calling me Robbie."

"I don't know," my mother said giggling a little, "No matter how big you get, you'll always be little Robbie Starr to me." I swear, Rob could charm any woman of any age at any time.

I finished my waffle, brought my dish over to the sink, and headed out of the kitchen.

"Hey Mia," Rob said before I'd made it to the door "Are you coming with me to see my mom?"

Had Rob done this on purpose – asked me in front of my parents? I was cornered.

"Uh, yeah, I guess." I said stiffly.

"In like, 20 minutes or so?" He asked politely.

"Sure."

"Remember we're all having dinner together tonight," my mom said.

"If you're cooking Mrs.…I mean Calista, then I'll be here."

Seriously, he was going to make me barf. I turned and all but ran out of the kitchen.

When I got to the stairs I paused and glanced over at Rob's house keys laying on the small table there. I'm not sure what I was thinking. I'm not even sure if the whole thought had formed in my head yet. Was there something on his keys? Paint?

But then Rob was there.

"What's wrong?" he whispered loudly.

I ignored him and started up the stairs. He grabbed me by the wrist. I spun around and glared at him with a wudderyoucrazy expression on my face. Rob let go of me but followed me up the stairs and into my room – shutting the door behind him.

"What are you doing?" I asked

"Mia?" Rob said, sounding a little desperate.

"What?"

"You're mad."

"No, I'm not."

"Then why are you acting like this?"

"Like what?"

"Like…mad."

I sighed. I could feel the tears forming in my eyes. "I just… I don't know."

"Don't know what?" He looked at me innocently.

"I mean…I get it that you don't want to be with me all the time but last night…" I hesitated. I really wasn't sure what I wanted to say. No, wait, that's not true at all. I knew what I *wanted* to say. I wanted to say, 'but last night you acted like a complete asshole. You should have come and picked me up. You should have walked me home. It was dark and freezing cold. Something could have happened to me. And if you cared about me like you say you do you wouldn't have been such a selfish jerk.' That's what I wanted to say.

But I didn't. I couldn't. I couldn't say what I truly felt. I couldn't demand anything. Because I was the one with everything to lose. Sure, Rob said he cared about me and had a cute nickname for me and looked for me from the free throw line, but none of it mattered. He wasn't my boyfriend – not really. He was Rob Starr and I was Mia Morgan. We were not a couple. We were not equals. And I would always feel like I was somehow … cosmically blessed…to be with him; terrified every minute that if I asked for too much or made things too difficult for him than everything we had (whatever that was) would all disappear.

Then Rob said, "Who said I don't want to be with you all the time?"

I started to cry. I know, I know, but I couldn't help it. I was so exhausted and relieved that he still liked me that the tears just came out.

Rob walked over and put his arms around me. "Please don't cry Mia. And please don't be mad at me anymore. I never want you to be mad at me." Rob's words caught in his throat as if he might cry too. "There's just so much shit going on and sometimes I just feel like… I'm going crazy and I just want to… I don't know. And you're like, the only real person I know. The only person I can be myself with. I want us to be even closer than we are now. You know that."

He pulled me towards him, and I let him. Then we stood there and hugged and breathed together and I felt this ache of happiness in my chest – like that feeling when you're a kid and you've cried so hard that you almost feel good – exhausted but sort of cozy.

"I'm so happy you're not moving out," I said

"Me too," said Rob, "but maybe that wouldn't be such a bad thing."

I tried to pull back from him, but he held me closer.

"If we moved back in with my dad," he continued into my hair, "then maybe in a couple of weeks, we could finally tell people about us."

"Really?"

"Of course, really."

And then we were kissing, and it was like we couldn't get close enough to each other. But of course, we had to stop. Anyone could walk in… I forced myself to move to the other side of the bed, so I wouldn't touch him. "Tonight…" Rob started to say but then someone knocked and we both sort of jumped even though we were already standing several feet away from each other. It was Jake. He looked embarrassed and miserable as usual. "Mr. Morgan is ready to take us to the rehab center."

I'm sure you can imagine how happy I was that day – and I was – really. But since I have promised you total honesty here, there was one thing that was itching at the back of my brain. It was about Rob of course and if you had asked me right there and then if I was thinking it, I would not have admitted it – or maybe wouldn't have even realized it. But, despite what Rob said about how I was the only person he could be himself with and despite his amazing kisses and the rollercoaster feeling in my stomach and the sympathy I had for everything he was going through – in spite of all that – I kept thinking about what Rob hadn't said about the night before. He hadn't said he was sorry. He hadn't said that he'd never do something like that again. He hadn't even acknowledged the fact that he'd done anything wrong at all. He just didn't want me to be mad at him anymore. And even though Rob had just told me he wanted to tell people about us (someday) and everything was awesome or at least seemed awesome and even felt awesome, I still didn't feel sure of anything.

CHAPTER 27

"It"

January 10ᵗʰ

L ate that night, after our big "family" dinner Rob sneaked into my room and climbed into bed with me. It was the first time we had ever been that daring or stupid or whatever, and, as you might imagine, things got very hot and heavy. Not like it was out of the blue or anything – I mean things had been progressing steadily in that department – but because most of our sex life took place in the dining room of my house, so I was always slowing things down. We never did things... real things... like stuff that required us to re- move our clothes. Just being in bed together, less than half dressed and touching each other however we wanted to, was further than we'd ever gone before. And (warning – some graphic detail here) eventually Rob got off (you know, had an orgasm) which happened through combination of me touching him and then him sort of fin- ishing things since I really didn't know how. And it was strange – or... not strange but, you know, something I'd never experienced before. But most of it was kind of fun and Rob seemed happy.

Before Rob had left my room that night, we'd agreed on a plan. Next Sunday – which happened to be the day after my sixteenth birthday – was Hallie and Rachel's fourth grade assembly which meant that both my parents and Mr. Starr would have to be there. And it just so happened that Jake had hockey try-outs that same afternoon. This meant that Rob and I would have the whole house to ourselves for at least three hours. I think you know what I'm getting at here.

The week was super busy. I had two tests and a quiz (79, 85, and 84, if you must know). Rob had an away game on Saturday, so, with all the practices and stuff, I barely saw him during the week. When we did see each other, we were oddly polite and tentative and maybe a little scared of each other and what we were about to do. At least that was true for me anyway. I couldn't really imagine what Rob had to be afraid of; but for me, well, it was my first time and I was mildly terrified.

My birthday came without much fanfare. I went out to dinner with my family and Rachel (of course). Both Rob and Jake were at the basketball game, which was way upstate, so they didn't get home until after eleven.

And then it was Sunday. The morning flew by in a flurry of the usual last-minute errands and 'Mommy, I can't find my…' and 'honey, did you remember to…' and then my parents and the girls were finally out the door. Jake was the last to leave the house and maybe it was just my imagination, but I swear he knew. When his ride showed up, he looked at me like he was leaving me behind on a sinking ship. I just gave him a 'what's your problem' face and he turned away, banging his bulky hockey bag against the doorframe as he left.

As soon as the door closed, the house fell strangely silent. Rob must have felt it too because he whispered when he spoke.

"So, are you still up for this?"

I nodded. I was. Or at least I was pretty sure I was. I loved Rob and I knew Rob really wanted to and we'd done a lot of other stuff already and it seemed sort of inevitable, so why wait? Besides, what did "ready" really feel like anyway? I mean who's ever really ready to lose their virginity? Okay, stupid question. I'm sure plenty of people are – like for instance, every guy on earth. And probably all those people who wait for marriage. But for most everyone else – how are they really sure?

I followed Rob up the stairs to my bedroom. Not my actual bedroom – not the one Rob and Jake now shared – but the guest room that I currently lived in. There was a red rose on the pillow. So, okay, you probably know me well enough by now to have figured out that I'm not the kind of girl who goes for stuff like single red roses on pillows – or flower petals – or stuffed animals holding hearts. But Rob didn't really get that about me (obviously). And sure, maybe the first time a guy did those things for a girl it was romantic, but by the eighty millionth time you've seen it in a cheesy movie or a reality TV show, it just felt like something you checked off on a list. Condom – check, soft music – check, rose on pillow – check. Yet there it was and well, "aw", is all I can say. It was sweet. Not the cliché rose itself but the idea that Rob had to sneak the rose into the house somehow and into my room – that kind of effort is romantic – I had to give him that.

"Are you okay?" he whispered.

"You don't have to whisper," I said, my voice sounding far too loud in the quiet room. "On second thought…" I whispered, and Rob laughed.

I sat down next to him with my legs draped over his and we started kissing. We were good at kissing. We had been from the start. But everything seemed a little different this time. Rob seemed overly anxious and I was hesitant. 'Relax' I told myself, but it just wasn't flowing right. Rob reached up and started unbuttoning my shirt.

"Wait," I said.

"What?"

"It's too light in here." I got up and walked across the room to pull the curtain. I was uncomfortably aware that Rob was watching me.

When I sat back down, he said, "Better?"

I nodded, and we resumed kissing.

It was better – not perfect – but the darkened room felt safer and less revealing. Pretty soon we both had our shirts off. Rob's body was beautiful – muscular and smooth. He moved me around, so he was on top of me and I could feel... everything.

We started grinding at this point. I know it's an awful word – almost as bad as tits – maybe worse. But would you prefer dry humping because that's just beyond awful. Let's suffice to say we were both getting pretty worked up. Then Rob stopped. He sat to one side of me and undid his jeans. I felt like I was supposed to help him or something (again, saw this in a movie) but I just couldn't bring myself to do it. He pulled his pants off and kicked them to the floor so all he had on was green checked boxer shorts and white sweat socks. He looked at me for a moment and smiled. I pulled him back towards me and we were kissing again. After another minute or so, he moved his hand to the front of my pants and undid the button. He struggled a bit with the zipper.

"Here, I've got it," I said. I unzipped my pants and pulled them off with Rob watching me the entire time.

I could tell he was really into it now because his breath grew heavier. "You are so beautiful," he said pulling me towards him.

My heart was pounding against him. Partly because I was excited, but I think more because I was suddenly nervous as hell.

I lay down beside Rob and we started kissing again but it was weird because there were too many pillows, so we couldn't quite get on the same level. I was kind of smooshed between them. Rob tried to get a different angle by moving himself sort of half on top of me but then his arm was on my hair and it really hurt so I reached up to try to move it, but my elbow poked him in the eye.

"Oh my God, are you okay?" I said.

"I don't know," he said. "I might lose this eye."

We both laughed nervously. But then it was suddenly awkward – neither one of us knowing how to get back into it. Finally, I said, "Yeah? that's what he said."

It was a stupid joke, but I guess that's what was funny about it because we both started cracking up. We laughed so hard there were tears in our eyes. And when our laughing subsided, and we were kind of out of breath Rob leaned over and traced my cheek and mouth with his finger.

"I've never been like this with anyone," he whispered, and I knew what he meant. We had these moments – like the laughing – when we just connected – when were just ourselves. Maybe it was because we'd known each other since we were little or maybe it was because we were so different. We didn't fit into his world or mine, so we made our own.

We started kissing again and it was different now, calmer but more intense – more like it was supposed to be. And it felt incredible – being practically naked – his skin against mine – the idea of second base or third base dissolving into something more fluid and graceful. Rob's fingers found their way inside my underwear and when I touched him in turn, he groaned. Eventually he pulled back and asked me if I was ready. I nodded.

Rob pulled off his underwear and was naked. For the record it was the first time I'd ever seen a boy or man or whatever – a guy – totally naked and aroused (yet another ridiculous word).

"Uh, the socks too …" I said.

"Yes, Ma'am," he said, laughing, but I could tell he was nervous.

Once his socks were off, he leaned towards me and kissed me softly on the mouth. Then he helped me pull off my underwear and slid his body onto mine. He kissed my neck just beneath my ear. "I love you," he whispered. His voice was rough, and his face was a little scratchy. And I didn't say it back. Not that I didn't feel it because I was sure I did, but I thought it might sound fake if I said it right then, like I'd only said it because he did; and maybe I was a bit distracted by what we were about to do.

And then we did it. Well, eventually we did it. We had to try a few times because it kind of hurt so I kept making him stop. But then we did do it. And I would tell you every detail – I know I promised not to lie about anything – but some things are just a little too private and some are simply too anatomical to share – the condom part for instance was not a particularly magical mo- ment. But what I will tell you is that it wasn't terrible. In fact, it felt nice, and I don't know…natural. So okay, that's obvious – I mean it's obviously natural, but I remember when I first learned about what sex was and I was kind of like "really?". Why would anyone want to do that?' But when Rob and I were doing it, it seemed normal. Like once it was happening my body seemed to accept the idea. The other thing I will share is that there weren't any acrobatics of any kind. We weren't rolling around, changing positions like you see in the movies. Rob was on top of me and stayed there the whole time, which, by the way, was under three minutes. And if I'm going for as much truth as possible here, then I have to admit that while it felt good (eventually), it didn't feel *great* – at least not for me. I mean everything leading up to *it* felt kind of great. But the actual intercourse part hurt – not ter- ribly, but some – and, well, it was more than just that. Or maybe

I should say it was less than that. And then it was over. And Rob was really, really happy.

We lay there for a few minutes, neither of us knowing exactly what to do next. And it wasn't like the movies where the couple is all sweaty like they've just run a marathon and it wasn't all cuddly and lovey either. We just kind of lay there – without saying anything and honestly, all I could think about was that my parents would be coming home soon and if we'd gotten the sheets dirty.

Finally, I said, "We should…"

"Yup," Rob agreed quickly. "But just one more thing." Rob rolled over and opened my bedside table drawer. He reached in and pulled out a small, unwrapped box with a blue bow stuck to the top.

"Happy birthday," he whispered.

Inside the box was a tiny silver ring with a lower-case b on it and I don't know if it was the situation – having just had sex for the first time, which if I didn't say already, is a seriously emotional thing – or how sweet and personal and thoughtful the gift was – but I burst into tears.

"Oh God, you hate it." Rob said, knowing full well that I didn't.

I shook my head furiously. "I love it so much!" I sobbed.

And I did. It was the best present I'd ever gotten, even though I knew instantly I could never wear it. I mean, everyone knew Rob called me little b. If they saw the ring, they would totally figure out we were more than friends. But I loved it anyway. I tied it around my Christmas bear's neck with a green ribbon (Ellsworth colors).

● ● ●

So, that was it, my first time; my first and *only* first time – because you know, you only get one. And okay, you already knew that, but have you ever really thought about it? Have you ever considered that it will be your "first time" story for your entire life? Me either.

Turns out there were four other important things I hadn't considered – and maybe, definitely, should have – before I had sex.

First. It turns out once you've had sex, you can't un-have it. Okay, so that sounds really obvious but there's more to it than that. You see if the person you had sex with is your boyfriend (or girlfriend) then they'll pretty much expect you to continue to have sex from that point forward and will be very confused and maybe even pissed off if you don't want to. I mean, you did it already, so what's the big deal? Right? Not that I wanted to stop having sex with Rob, I just didn't really think about this ahead of time and I soon realized there was no going backwards.

Then there's the pregnancy thing. And yes, you already knew this one too – duh. But what you might not know is that when you start having sex with someone sort of regularly – even if you are using birth control religiously – which we were – you are going to worry EVERY MONTH until you get your period. And if you're late, you'll be basically terrified until it finally (hopefully) comes.

And maybe the most confusing thing I learned was that sex isn't always as simple for girls as it is for guys. What I'm trying to say – in more explicit terms – is that most guys have a way easier time having orgasms than most girls do. WAY. EASIER. At least that was the case for me and yeah, sure, there probably are some girls out there somewhere who can have one just sitting on the washing machine or bike riding or whatever urban legend you've heard, but after some googling on the subject – I can safely say – most cannot. Of course, the internet also has plenty of suggestions on how to solve that problem along with a bunch of pop-up ads you really don't want your parents to see. However, when you have just-turned sixteen and your boyfriend is the most gorgeous and popular boy in school – and yeah, I'm talking about me now – I was not quite ready to go make suggestions and certainly not demands. Honestly, I wasn't even sure what I was supposed to ask for. Plus, I was worried he might think there was something wrong with what we were already doing, and there wasn't. Everything we were doing felt great, very great, it was just, well, not as great for me as it was for him.

Which brings me to the last thing I learned, which is sex doesn't really change anything. If the person you are having sex with doesn't love or respect you before you've had sex, he or she is probably not going to start loving and respecting you afterwards. However, if they *do* love and respect you, I think they probably will continue to after you've done it. The tricky part is knowing whether or not they are telling the truth before it all goes down.

CHAPTER 28

What Kind of Person Does That?

January 12ᵗʰ

That's all I'm going to say on the subject of sex, except that Rob and I were now having sex as often as we could – which wasn't easy given someone else was always home or Rob was at practice or we had to go visit his mom. A couple of times, I let him sneak into my room in the middle of the night, but it was never much fun. I was always too terrified of getting caught to enjoy it.

But I'm getting ahead of myself here. Because something important happened over those next several days starting with the Tuesday after the Sunday that Rob and I had sex.

I got a text. I know that doesn't sound like big news but in my case, it was. The text was from Carmen. It said.

Eric saw Rob and his friends keying those cars last week.

And then another.

Yesterday some of them cornered him in the gym and told him if he told anyone they would kill him. Then they threw basketballs at him until he was almost unconscious. He had to go to the hospital.

And then...

Thought you should know.

I wish I could tell you that I didn't believe it. Or that I thought Carmen was making it up or something. But the truth is, I did believe it. I sort of just knew it was true. I certainly knew Justin was capable of doing stupid things. But up until then, I thought it was only vandalism. I also knew Rob had been under a lot of stress and that's just the way some kids blow off steam. Right? I mean vandalism was stupid, but a lot of kids did it and thought it was funny. And no one really got hurt. But this was different.

I also wish I could tell you that I did something about it; something brave or kind or smart. But I didn't.

I couldn't. If I told someone what Rob and his friends had done, they'd take it out on Eric. I couldn't risk Eric getting hurt again. But of course, that's not the whole truth, is it? As horrible as it sounds, I didn't tell anyone because I knew if I did, Rob would never forgive me. It would ruin everything.

So, I ignored it. I deleted the text. I did nothing.

I felt horrible. I felt sort of sick or like maybe I was going insane. I mean, I knew I was wrong, yet I was willing to live with that as long as it meant that I could still have Rob. What kind of person does that?

Me.

CHAPTER 29

Don't Call Me Chloe

January 24th

S o, you would think that now that Rob and I were having sex I'd feel surer of myself with him. But unfortunately, it didn't work that way. We were still lying to everyone – pretending we weren't a couple – and now the lie was even bigger. I mean, come on. You shouldn't have to pretend you're not in a relationship with the person you're having sex with.

Which leads me to the following Saturday.

Normally, Rob and I (and sometimes Jake) would go see his mother on Saturdays but Jake was at a friend's house and Rob was at Arcade Mania with his basketball buddies for Team Appreciation Day. I'd planned on spending my day doing homework, but the truth is, I was on my phone tracking all the fun everyone else was having and going stir crazy. So, at about three-thirty, I gave up on my homework, and asked my dad for a ride to the rehab center to visit Mrs. Gerber-Starr on my own.

It was one of those gloomy January days. The rehab parking lot was nearly empty, dirty snow piles crammed into the corners of the vacant spaces. The building looked dark, and I wondered for a minute if it was closed. But, as I crossed the pavement towards the entrance, the electronic doors slid open, and for a moment no one appeared. Then out of the darkness stepped Chloe Olson, her white parka glowing in the gray afternoon. She was looking down at her phone as she walked towards me, so it was several seconds before she realized I was there.

"Oh, hey!" she said. A flicker of a something – amusement? – crossed her face. "What are you doing here?"

I shook my head and forced a smile. "I'm here to see Mrs. Gerber-Starr. Me and... my mom come to visit a lot."

"That is like, *so* nice. They were like, really good friends, right?"

"Yes, they are," I said.

"Yeah, it's like, super sad." Chloe shook her head. "She looks...and her hair...well...hopefully she'll, you know, get better soon."

"Yeah."

"Gotta go. See you tomorrow."

"Bye."

Chloe walked past me, and I forced myself to move. I stepped through the sliding doors silently willing them to hurry up and close behind me. My throat felt tight and my breath was shallow. What the hell was Chloe doing there? Sure, Chloe and Mrs. G-S must know each other. Chloe and Rob had gone out for a long time – years – so maybe they were friends or something. Maybe Chloe was just visiting Mrs. G-S to be nice. But still.

That was the last thought I had before I turned into Mrs. Gerber-Starr's room. Rob was sitting on the far side of the bed – his back to the door. It took me a full ten seconds to say something.

"Hi," I said quietly so as not to startle Mrs. G-S.

Rob spun around. "Mia...hi...what are you doing here?"

"I came to visit your mom."

"Wow… yeah, sure, of course."

"I thought…I was worried that no one was coming today."

"Yeah, that was nice of you. Me too. I mean, I was worried too. I didn't think I was going to be able to come – you know, the team day thing and everything. But then…"

I crossed behind Rob to where Mrs. Gerber-Starr was sitting in wheelchair by the window. I took her hand and she smiled vaguely at me. "Then, what?" I asked without turning around to look at Rob. I waited; my breath held tight in my chest.

"Well, then I thought I would because it ended early."

I nodded. I was so mad that I felt dizzy. He wasn't going to say anything about Chloe being here. He was going to lie – to hide it from me. Why? Did he feel guilty? Should he feel guilty?

I couldn't make myself look at him, so I busied myself adjusting the pillow behind Mrs. Gerber-Starr's back.

Okay, this wasn't the end of the world. Maybe it was just totally innocent. Maybe I was crazy. It wasn't like I caught them kissing or something. Maybe Rob just didn't tell me because he didn't want me to get upset. But then Mrs. Gerber-Starr patted my hand, "Thank you, Chloe dear," she said.

Before I even knew what I was doing, I had crossed the room and bolted down the hall. I wasn't even sure why I was so mad. I just was. I was just so sick of it – of being alone all the time, of pretending everything was normal. I was sick of everyone getting to be with Rob but me. Pathetic as it was, visiting his mother was one of the few things we had that was ours – without basketballers or Baditudes – and now Chloe was going to be there, too?

And why did Mrs. G-S have to go and call me Chloe? Oh sure, I knew that she was confused and everything, and I knew that Chloe had just been there so that probably messed her up, but I had been going to see her for weeks, months, and she'd known me since I was practically a baby. Why didn't she recognize me? Or maybe she just wished I was Chloe. Maybe she thought Chloe was better than me – better for Rob.

I wasn't sure what to do. I had no ride, so I headed towards the high school – sort of walk-running the whole way. By the time, I'd gone the almost half mile to get there, my tears had practically frozen to my face. I tried the parking lot doors, but they were locked. I walked around the building trying every door. It was getting dark. I took out my phone to call my dad.

But then Rob was there. "What the fuck, Mia?" he said. He was out of breath, as if he'd been running. "I been looking everywhere for you."

"I saw her." I said, new tears warming my frozen cheeks.

"Who?" Rob demanded. His hands were jammed in his pockets, his shoulders raised.

"Who do you think?" I snapped.

"Chloe? Is that what this is about? Chloe?" He laughed – not really a laugh – more like a 'ha'. "She's just a friend. It's no big deal. I've told you before. You don't have to worry about her."

"You've never told me that before." I said. "And I do have to worry. She still likes you."

"Okay, well, I'm telling you now. And she doesn't still like me. She's hanging out with Reynolds now. And she dumped *me* – remember?"

"Well, so…she shouldn't be visiting your mom. I mean she's not your girlfriend, right? I am…I'm your stupid, secret, invisible girlfriend that no one knows about except your mother, kind of, and now she thinks I'm Chloe."

"She doesn't think you're Chloe. She's just confused. And you are my girlfriend. Even if no one else knows. I know."

I started to cry again. I was just really tired – tired of all the worrying and all the hours of obsessing, tired of not ever feeling like I could just relax and be myself.

"I love you, Mia," Rob said. "What can I do to make you believe me?"

I shrugged and wiped my face on my coat sleeve.

Rob pulled his hands from his pockets and spread his arms to the sky. "I love Mia Morgan" he shouted. Do you hear me, world? Look," he said grabbing my phone and turning it on himself. "I love Mia Morgan" he shouted again.

Suddenly, the lights in the parking lot went on.

I squealed in surprise and we both laughed.

Rob went to shout again but I rushed over to him. "Shhhh. Someone will hear you!" I said tugging his arms down to his sides, but he put them around me instead.

"I love you, Mia. Me and Chloe: we were never as close as everyone thinks. She was always mad about something or had some drama going on. She's a total bitch. She would say she loved me then flirt with other guys to make me…"

I stopped Rob with a kiss but not because I wanted to kiss him. It was because I couldn't listen to him talk about her anymore. I couldn't stand hearing what he was going to say next. Because I wished with all my heart that I could somehow unhear everything he'd already said. I didn't want to know that he was the one who'd been dumped and hurt and not the other way around. I didn't want to know how jealous he was when she flirted with other guys.

And sure, he'd declared his love for me at the top of his lungs in the school parking lot, but we both knew that in the late hours of that bleak afternoon, no one heard him but me.

We walked back to my/ our house together. It was freezing, and I had to pee. And even though Rob seemed happy in a proud-of-himself sort of way, I felt strange. Changed. Older. I had that hollowed out feeling in my chest – like when I discovered all the toys on my Christmas list piled in the back of my mom's closet waiting to be wrapped. There were some things you wish you never knew or never had to know.

Don't get me wrong. I wasn't over him. I didn't stop worshipping him and I certainly wasn't done obsessing about him. But I remember a sense that something had shifted in me that afternoon. That no matter how much I wanted to, I couldn't do it anymore. How long could we keep going around and around, fighting and making up without anything really changing? How long could I keep tricking myself into believing my ears and not my heart? Because even though Rob said all the right things, I didn't feel them – not the way you're supposed to feel them. Sadly, at the time, this new realization only made me more desperate to hold on to him, to the idea of him, of us, even knowing that the tighter I grasped at our relationship, the more likely it was to be crushed by my own hands.

Ellsworth High School Case #1141
Transcript of interview: March 22
Student: Mia Morgan
Counselor: Dr. Janis Dubrovski

Dr. Dubrovski: *What about the Starr boys?*

Mia Morgan: *What? What about them?*

Dr. Dubrovski: *Well, could this have something had to do with them?*

Mia Morgan: *No, why? Why would you ask that?*

Dr. Dubrovski: *Well, there is some speculation that the boys in the photographs are possibly boys from the basketball team and, of course, if that is the case, they would know Rob Starr. And, as you know, both Rob and Jake Starr have had a ...troubled year. Maybe one of them had something to do with this. Maybe there something going on with you and Jake, perhaps?*

Mia Morgan: *No (laughs). There's nothing going on with me and Jake Starr.*

CHAPTER 30

Weird

February 5th

A few more weeks went by and once again, I saw very little of Rob. Basketball season was coming to an end and the team wasn't doing well enough to guarantee a spot in the playoffs. This meant that every game mattered. Rob was pushing the guys hard and himself even harder.

Whenever I did see Rob, which was mostly at our tutoring sessions, Rob talked almost exclusively about basketball. It was as if Rob had ORD about basketball the way I had ORD about him. Okay maybe it wasn't as bad as Obsessive Repulsive Disorder, but it was annoying. He was constantly inventing hypothetical problems – what if he or one of the better players got injured? What if Reynold's got kicked off the team because of his C in Physics? And of course, what if they *did* make the finals but his Mom wasn't recovered enough to come, which, for him, was bigger than all the other worries put together.

And speaking of Mrs. G-S, in the last few weeks, she had started to make real progress again. She was finally able to have the surgery on her leg, which had been delayed until she could handle the physical therapy necessary for it to be successful.

While this was great news, the intense physical therapy meant more trips to the rehab center – something Rob didn't have time for – and more interactions with Mr. Starr – something Rob and Jake had been carefully avoiding since the revelation that he'd been having an affair with his business colleague.

Then there was school, which, speaking as his Trig tutor, Rob should have been more worried about. But, for Rob, compared to basketball and his mom, grades were the least of his concerns.

On top of everything, or perhaps because of it, Rob was partying a lot more on the weekends and even sometimes on school nights, leaving even less time for us. The truth was, at this point, our relationship basically consisted of Trig study sessions (with very little studying going on), me going to games whenever I could (watching Rob but not really interacting with him), and Rob sneaking into my room at night – more often than he should – half drunk (or sometimes all drunk) so we could fool around.

At the time, I acted like this was okay with me, like it was romantic or cute or something. But it wasn't, really. Rob was horny and sloppy and smelled of beer, and we couldn't talk above a whisper or turn on the lights for fear my parents would wake up. Honestly, sometimes in the dark, late at night, when Rob would wake me up, I'd get the weirdest feeling – like it wasn't really me in the bed with him. Or not me specifically. I was just someone, a body, another way to distract himself. But I couldn't say no. I never said no. I told myself it was my responsibility to care for him. I was his girlfriend and that's what girlfriends do. He was under so much pressure and I was supposed to be there for him. So, I let it happen and keep happening because deep down I feared… I knew… that if it wasn't me, it would be someone else.

Then, one Thursday night, two extremely weird things happened. My parents had taken Hallie and Rachel to the annual fourth grade field trip to see a Broadway play. Rob was at an away game a few towns north of ours with one of Ellsworth's main rivals, the Port Windsor Wombats. Sally Verma caught a ride with some of Veronica's friends so I ended up stuck at home alone.

It was about nine-thirty or so when I heard Jake come in. I was upstairs studying for Social Studies, but I knew it had to be Jake. It was too early for my parents to be back, and Rob and his friends usually hung out after the games. I heard the TV go on in the den – some stupid sitcom – the sound of canned laughter drifted up the stairs. And normally I would have just left him down there alone – Jake and I had gotten good at ignoring one another's presence – but I heard a loud thump, followed by a groan and then lot of swearing.

It was none of my business but for some reason I thought that maybe I should do something in case he was hurt or something. Ever since the whole stuff with his dad's affair came out, I kind of felt bad for him. I mean, of course I felt bad for him, but I guess I sort of understood better why he'd been acting like such a jerk.

So, because of the loud noise and my charitable mood, and maybe because I was a little bored, I decided to go downstairs. For the record, I was kind of a mess that night. I mean I was clean and all, in fact I'd just gotten out of the shower. But my hair was still damp and wavy, which looked terrible; or maybe not terrible, but not as good as it looked straight. And since it was just me home, there really wasn't any reason to straighten my hair until the morning. Anyway, the point was, my hair was messy, and I had no makeup on and I was in my "pajamas" which was basically an old t-shirt and boxer shorts. Not that it matters what I was wearing but I just don't want you to get the wrong idea – like I was trying to look cute or anything because I really, *really* wasn't.

I headed into the kitchen and got some corn chips and, in a gesture to be nice, two glasses of lemonade, but when I walked into the family room and put the lemonade down if front of Jake I saw that something was wrong. Jake was drunk. Not just buzzed, but full-on drunk – like the kind of drunk you see people act out on TV. He looked like hell and he smelled worse.

"Hey," I said. "Are you alright?"

His head swiveled to look at me. He scowled.

"Are you drunk?" It was a stupid question, I'll admit.

"No." His eyes were red and puffy, and his cheeks had that streaky, tear-tracked look that little kids get when they've been crying.

"Okay, well, maybe you should go upstairs and take a shower or something. My parents are going to be home pretty soon."

He got up and, for a minute, I thought he was going to do what I'd suggested, but instead he went into the kitchen. I heard the refrigerator door open and then the sound of a bottle opener and the tumble of the metal cap as it landed on the counter. He came back into the den with a beer and sat down on the couch. He took a big swallow and burped loudly.

This was not good. I was sure my parents were already stressed out enough just managing the Mrs. Gerber-Starr situation and the Mr. Starr affair thing and the Jake getting in trouble at school stuff. I don't know if they could handle Jake drinking in their living room. They might even decide to reverse their reverse decision and make the Starrs move out this time.

I didn't know what to do but I couldn't just leave him there, so I sat down and turned my attention to the TV.

Jake was watching some old Disney show – one of those stupid and predictable and completely-unfunny-yet-for-some-reason-you-can't-stop-watching-them kind of shows. We sat there for a minute or two until I suddenly became conscious of the fact that Jake wasn't looking at the TV anymore but was looking at me instead. My mouth was half full of chips.

"What's up?" I said trying to sound like it was normal that he was drunk and watching me eat chips.

"Your hair…" he paused; his expression was serious. "Your hair looks better like that."

"Uh…thanks," I said waiting for some rude follow up to the comment. Jake wasn't exactly famous for his charm.

"No, really. You look more like you. You should wear it like that all the time."

"Sure…yeah." I said. I looked over at him. He had turned his attention to the bottle of beer in his hand.

"Jake, are you okay?" I asked. "I mean you're acting like… you're drinking a beer in the house on a school night. What's going on? Not that I blame you for being, you know…upset or anything. I know it must be awful for you with everything going on with your mom and your dad."

Jake shrugged, not looking up from the bottle.

"I guess, well, I can't even imagine," I said. I'm not sure what had gotten into me, but I couldn't seem to stop talking. "Rob's having a hard time too, you know. But you know him, he doesn't like to talk about it. And you know, I totally get it. If you don't want to talk about it – that's fine. I just …I mean we don't really know each other that well anymore but I want you to know that I feel bad about what's happening to you guys."

Jake nodded. "Thanks Mia. That was a reallanicespeech," he slurred. "I'll be sure to tell Rob what an awesome *friend* you are."

Okay, so what did that mean? Was he trying to tell me that he knew that Rob and I were a thing? Did he think I was only saying that stuff so it would get back to Rob? It was weird and not very nice. I got up.

"Whatever." I said. "You don't always have to be such a douche, you know?" I picked up my glass and the bowl of chips and headed into the kitchen. Jake followed me.

"I'm a douche? You hang out with Rob and you think *I'm* a douche?"

"Yeah, 'cuz you kind of are," I said. I turned my back to him and rinsed my lemonade glass and opened the dishwasher.

"Mia…" he said, suddenly earnest, "if you knew half the stuff…if I told you what he did…he's *so* totally spoiled. He…"

"He, what?" I demanded.

"I don't know. I'm not saying…." Then he paused as if he didn't know what to say next.

"Yeah well…" I put my glass in the dishwasher leaned down to pull the door shut. When I stood up, Jake was right next to me.

"C'mon, Mia, I'm sorry. Please don't be mad."

"You know what, Jake…" I started. And I'd planned to say – 'you're drunk, and I know you're going through a lot of stuff, but you just can't be a jerk to everyone' – but I didn't get all the way through because before I could finish the sentence Jake was kissing me – or at least trying to kiss me. He'd leaned in and I stepped back (of course), which made him lose his balance (because he was drunk) and fall into me so his lips sort of missed mine and because I was in the middle of talking my mouth was half open and his lips, which were kind of cold and wet, connected with the side of my mouth and my cheek and well, the whole thing was just mortifyingly wrong.

We both stood there stunned for a few seconds until I turned and practically ran out of the room.

Several minutes later I heard Jake come upstairs. My door was locked but he didn't try to get in. I listened as he stumbled down the hall and I heard him go in the bathroom. He must have left the door open because I could hear him peeing for like twenty minutes. Then I heard the door of my old bedroom open and close. I even heard the bedsprings squeak as he fell heavily onto the mattress.

When I was sure he was asleep, I crept downstairs and quickly cleaned up. I dumped the untouched lemonade and what was left of the beer into the sink and sprayed some room freshener to hide the skunky smell. It was lucky I did because just as I was finishing up, I heard a key in the front door lock. Fortunately, it was Rob but get this – he was drunk too – and smelled. But not of beer.

CHAPTER 31

Weirder

February 5th continued

So, if the Jake part of the night wasn't weird enough...Rob came in and like I said, he was drunk. Okay so that isn't *that* weird, and he wasn't *that* drunk – certainly not as drunk as Jake. The weird part was, he smelled of gasoline.

"Hey," I said cautiously.

"Mia...good, you're home."

Where else did he think I would be? I wondered. But I could tell Rob wasn't really thinking clearly. He was amped up and distracted. He tossed his gym bag on the ground, then picked it up again and sniffed it.

"What's going on?" I asked tentatively.

"Shit."

"Rob, what's happening?"

"Nothing. It's just nothing...but I may need your help okay?"

"Yeah. Sure, Of course." Neither of us spoke while Rob pulled his sweatshirt off and then his uniform shirt.

"Can we do some laundry?"

"Now?"

"Yeah, now."

"Sure, but what's going on?" Rob pulled a few more articles of clothing out of his gym bag then turned it over and dumped the rest of the contents on the ground.

"Can we put this in the laundry too?" he asked holding up the bag itself.

"Uh, I think so, but hey," I put my hand on his arm to get him to focus. "What's happening?"

Rob took a deep breath and nodded. "So… we lost…but it was like, totally fucked. There was this one forward who fouled like three of our guys and the ref made like, two really bad calls against *us* instead of the asshole who was fouling everyone. Then we find out after the game that the ref was like this kid's cousin or uncle or something."

"Wow," I said, but I wasn't really listening. I was watching Rob. I'd never seen him so agitated. His face was flushed, and he kept passing the gym bag back and forth between his hands like a basketball.

"And we told Coach and he said we could protest the game but when we did the Windsor kids were heckling us and being total dicks. They were talking shit about how we sucked, and we were pussies for protesting. And well that was just bullshit, you know? Every fucking year…" Rob shook his head in disgust. Then he paused and looked into my eyes. "Anyway, you just need to say that I got home around ten. Okay?"

"Okay… but you still haven't told me what happened."

"Mia," Rob said grabbing my hand. "You need to get this stuff in the washing machine, and I need to take a shower, okay? It's no big deal. I promise. Okay?"

I nodded. But that didn't mean I believed him.

● ● ●

Rob was freshly showered and eating cereal out of a mixing bowl (seriously, he and Jake could each eat a whole box in one sitting) by the time my parents got back. The sports channel blared loudly from the TV as it always did when Rob was home. Jake was upstairs asleep (I hoped), and even though it was a late evening at the Morgan household, everything seemed kind of normal.

My father went into the kitchen for a glass of water then joined Rob on the couch. Hallie and Rachel, who were still excited from their big night out, chattered happily about the show until my mother finally ushered them upstairs. She came back down a few minutes later to "set the house straight," which she always did before going to bed.

It was right about then that the doorbell rang. My father and mother looked at each other questioningly. Rob and I shot each other a look as well. His expression said, 'no big deal – got it?'

It was my dad who answered the door, and even though I had half expected it, it was still sort of shocking to see a police officer in your front hall – two actually – a woman and a man. The woman asked my father if Rob Starr lived on the premises.

For a moment, I froze. I thought, *this is it*. Rob's been caught doing something. He's going to get in trouble. And I was surprised to realize that I was relieved. It was as if, ever since Eric had been beaten up, I'd somehow been waiting – maybe even wishing – for this to happen without even knowing it. But I should have known it wasn't going to be that simple. Not when Rob Starr was involved.

After some establishing of who was who and why the Starr kids were staying with us, we finally got to the story. Officer Johns, who clearly loved her job and the lingo that went with it – explained that there was a fire in the equipment shed behind the football bleachers at Port Windsor High School. Some kids, MICs, (minors in consumption of alcohol, she explained) were spotted by an eyewitness.

According to the witness, the boys were dressed in Ellsworth team uniforms and had, allegedly (Officer John's word) loaded some sneakers with rocks, doused them with gasoline, lit them on fire, and tossed them through the storage facility windows. The building, equipment and even a portion of the bleachers were destroyed – an early estimate of approximately ten thousand dollars' worth of damage. On top of that, one of the janitors who had stayed late to clean up after the game had sustained injuries – including a severely burned hand – trying to put the fire out before the fire department arrived.

They (the police) were talking to everyone on the team, trying to get to the bottom of the whole thing.

I stood there trying as hard as I could not to look at Rob. Of course, I knew it was him and his stupid friends. Probably Justin and Mike or maybe Reynolds. No one said anything until my father spoke. "I'm sure Rob had nothing to do with this, Officer."

At this point, Rob spoke up. "No, ma'am," he said confidently. "No one on my team would *ever* do something like that."

It was amazing to witness – knowing (or at least sort of knowing) the truth – to watch Rob turn on the Rock Starr magic. Officer Johns, so certain she'd found her culprit, suddenly softened and looked concerned.

The other officer spoke. "Yes son, I know it's hard to believe that someone would do something so irresponsible, especially you boys from our team, that's why we need everyone's cooperation to find out what really happened here. So, I'm sorry to have to ask this, but where were you tonight after the game?"

"I just came home. We lost, so there was no reason to stick around and celebrate. My friend Reynolds gave me a ride… Reynolds Prince." Rob paused making sure the cops heard Reynolds' name clearly. Reynolds' dad was a big shot in Ellsworth. "I've been here for a while."

"Can anyone attest to that." This from Officer Johns.

"I...can," I offered, glancing over at Rob. "We've been here watching TV."

"Did you have anything to drink tonight, son?"

Rob looked down at the floor and then he glanced up at my mom. His face embarrassed, apologetic.

"I, uh...yes. I had two beers in the car on the way home."

"Rob?" This from my mother.

"I'm sorry Mrs. Morgan," Rob said sincerely. "We just needed to...you know... It's not like we were drunk or anything, and Reynolds didn't drink at all because he was driving."

Officer Johns nodded seriously. "You know underage drinking is against the law, don't you, Rob? And so is the presence of open cans, bottles or other unsealed containers of alcoholic beverages inside a moving vehicle."

"I know. It was stupid. I don't know what we were thinking."

It was weird – and a bit disturbing – how Rob seemed to have everything under control. I mean, he was so convincing it was almost creepy. He told the truth about the beer (sort of) and it was brilliant; it made him seem so honest.

At that point Rob's phone, which was sitting on the coffee table behind us, buzzed – a text.

Officer Johns glanced over Rob's shoulder at the phone and then back to him. "Are you going to get that?" she asked.

Rob shrugged, "I'm sure it's nothing important."

Officer Johns nodded as though she understood something profound. Her expression shifted. "Where's your uniform, son?" She asked.

"Oh...I threw it in the wash. It was really gross and sweaty."

The officers exchanged a look.

"How about your sneakers? Can you show us those?"

My heart bounced up from my chest to the back of my throat. Was Rob wearing sneakers when he came in? I didn't think so – no – socks and some sort of black slide-ons, the kind that all the jocks wore in the showers. But Rob didn't hesitate.

"Uh… sure. I'll go get them."

Rob went upstairs and we all just stood there. Finally, my mother turned to my father and said. "We should probably call Bill and let him know what's going on."

"Well," my father said slowly, "maybe let's hold off until these officers have cleared this thing up. No need to worry Bill. I'm sure Rob's not involved."

At that point, Rob came bounding down the stairs with a pair of basketball sneakers in his hands. "Here they are," he said holding them out to the police.

Officer Johns took one of the shoes from him and turned it over. Then she held it up to her nose and sniffed.

"My, you're a brave woman," my mother said jokingly, nervously.

The officer handed the shoe to her partner and smiled as he smelled them too. "They're not that bad. My son's are far worse and he's only twelve. More importantly, I don't detect any gasoline. Rigotti?"

"Nope, nothing." Officer Rigotti handed the shoe back to Rob.

"I thought you said they threw the sneakers into the building?" my mother asked.

"Yes, that's correct," Officer Johns replied officially. "Two shoes were retrieved from the scene – completely destroyed – and those could have easily been stolen.

"Then why smell Rob's shoes?"

"Gasoline's messy, smelly stuff – usually splashes all over the place. I figure whoever the boys were, they'd likely get some on themselves as well."

My mother nodded in understanding.

Officer Johns turned to Rob. "I know no one wants to rat out their friends Rob, but if you or any of your buddies know anything about this, you need to come forward. We are going to find out who did this and if anyone lies or withholds information it will only make it worse."

Then she looked back and forth between Rob and me, her eyebrows lifted as if to say, "Are we clear?"

Rob nodded solemnly. "Yes ma'am."

I was enormously relieved when the police left, but while my father appeared to be convinced of Rob's innocence, my mother seemed a little suspicious. She asked Rob several more times if he knew of anyone who might have stayed after the game or who might have had a reason to do something so dangerous. Rob kept up his doe-eyed innocence, even proposing that the other team might have dressed up in Ellsworth uniforms to try and get our team in trouble. With that unlikely suggestion, my mother finally gave it a rest. But before she went upstairs, she reminded Rob again that lying about anything could get him in deeper trouble.

Rob never flinched. "I know, Mrs. Morgan... I mean Calista. You're right. I'll make sure the team does the right thing."

CHAPTER 32

The Other Sneaker

February 5ᵗʰ Late & February 6ᵗʰ

R ob and I stayed up after my parents went to bed, but we waited at least a half hour before either of us said anything. Finally, I asked, "Were you…I mean did you?"

Rob shook his head which at first I took to mean 'no' but then he said, "This whole thing is so stupid. They're making a huge deal out of it. What did that cop say? 'Ten thousand dollars' worth of stuff? I bet nothing even got ruined, there probably wasn't even anything in there. The police around here are so bored they'd turn a parking ticket into a federal case."

"But I mean did you guys..."

"Mia, the less we talk about this the better. If anyone asks, I was here watching TV with you. Okay?"

I nod.

Then Rob smiled and grabbed my hand. "Oh, hey, don't look so worried. It's no big deal. C'mere."

Rob and I kissed a little but neither one of us was really feeling it.

I went upstairs first, leaving Rob, texting, on the couch.

When I got to the top of the stairs, I was surprised to hear my parents were still up and it sounded like they were having an argument. I tiptoed nearer to their room.

"I'm simply saying that I don't think it's our responsibility." This from my mother.

My father must have been in their bathroom because his voice was a little muffled and I could hear water running. "It's not that big a deal, Calista. He had a couple of beers, he's seventeen years old. You were drinking beer when you were seventeen, weren't you?"

"That's not the point. The point is, if he's been drinking, and we didn't know it, what else is he doing that we don't know about? Doing drugs? Having sex? Haven't we had our hands full enough with Jake getting into fights at school and who knows what else with all the vandalism happening around town? We're not their parents and now something serious has happened and we shouldn't be the ones to decide how to handle it. It's not our job."

"There is nothing to handle. You heard him. He doesn't know anything about it."

"Really? Is that what you think? If that's the case, then why is his basketball uniform in the washing machine? The kid hasn't done a single load of laundry since he moved in and suddenly, he's a clean freak who can't stand the smell of sweat? Have you been in their room?"

My father turned off the faucet. "Well I don't know why he washed his uniform but apparently, his sneakers were fine." I could hear my father walking across the room nearer to where my mother was standing. His voice got softer. "He's a good kid Calista. Let's give him the benefit of the doubt."

My mother sighed loudly. "I do. I am. Really."

Despite what she said, I was worried. I knew my mother. She

genuinely cared about the community and doing the right thing. If she thought something was important, she wasn't going to just let it go. If she had a real reason to suspect Rob was involved, who knew what she'd do.

• • •

It didn't take long for the other shoe to fall – or in this case, the other sneaker. The next morning, Rob came down to breakfast early because, as he explained, he'd arranged an early morning meeting to talk to the team about the fire and try to figure out what happened. My mother said she thought that was very responsible of him, but again I sensed the doubt in her voice.

And then, just as Rob was about to go, Jake came downstairs. He was careful not to look at me as he walked into the kitchen and I realized suddenly that, in all the craziness, I'd completely forgotten about the awful almost-kiss.

"Has anyone seen my basketball sneakers?" he said.

I stopped breathing. I forced myself to keep my eyes on the toast I was buttering. What the hell?

"There are some out in the front hall," my mother said casually. "Are those them?" I swallowed hard. We all knew they were.

When Jake returned to kitchen, sneakers in hand, my mother turned to Rob. Her eyebrows raised questioningly.

Rob ran his hand through his hair and then sort of smiled. "I know what you must be thinking Mrs....er...Calista. But last night, when the police were here, I just ran upstairs and grabbed the first pair of sneakers I could find. I mean, Jake was asleep already, so I didn't want to turn on the light and I didn't want to keep the officers waiting. See?" he said pointing down at his feet, "I'm wearing mine now."

My mother and I both looked at Rob's feet and I'm sure I sighed out loud with relief.

"I know it looks kinda bad but really, that's what happened." Rob grabbed his books off the kitchen counter. "Now, I gotta run. You know…the team meeting. Sorry."

Seconds later the front door closed, and Jake said, "The police?"

Ellsworth High School Case #1141
Transcript of interview: March 22
Student: Mia Morgan
Counselor: Dr. Janis Dubrovski

Dr. Dubrovski: *So you don't deny you were drinking at the party?*

Mia Morgan: *Yes. I mean...no, I don't deny it. Everyone was drinking.*

Dr. Dubrovski: *And you went to the party alone.*

Mia Morgan: *Yes. I already told you that.*

Dr. Dubrovski: *And what did you wear that night?*

Mia Morgan: *What does that have to do with anything? Are you suggesting that I did something...that I brought this on somehow?*

Dr. Dubrovski: *No, I'm...no. But you must realize this is a serious situation. If these kids are identified or...well, these pictures could affect a lot of people – a lot of lives – not just yours.*

Mia Morgan: *What do you mean?*

Dr. Dubrovski: *I'm saying we're trying to understand the whole situation. And honestly, it concerns me that you won't tell us who these other kids are, when frankly, it's apparent you know. Are you considering taking matters into your own hands...planning some kind of revenge? Because if you are...well, really... it would really be best if you would just let us handle things.*

Mia Morgan: *Wait...you're worried about... them?*

CHAPTER 33

Guilty

February 6ᵗʰ

It was all anyone could talk about that day. Mostly about who did it and how the Port Windsor "assholes" deserved it. There was also a good deal of discussion about how much damage had been done – as in not nearly as much as the Port Windsor people were claiming – and that they were lucky that whoever did do it hadn't set their whole damn school on fire (which they deserved for being such assholes).

At around lunchtime someone from the local news station showed up with a camera and was trying to get kids to comment. Eventually the principal and the coach got them to leave but not before a few kids had been filmed saying they didn't know anything, but that whatever had happened, the Windsor kids had started it – which didn't exactly make the Ellsworth kids sound innocent. In spite of all the fuss, by the end of the day, it seemed as though the whole thing might just blow over. That is, until Mr. Starr showed up.

The news of Mr. Starr's appearance was all over the school in a matter of minutes. By the time I reached the main office there was already a crowd gathered outside. I'm not sure whose bright idea it was, sixty years ago, when the school was built, but the office was designed with walls that were half wall (at the bottom) and half window (at the top) – probably some kind of open environment kind of thinking. Anyway we could all see right in. Mr. Starr was talking to Principal Ryan. He was holding a plastic supermarket bag in one hand. I couldn't see Mr. Starr's face, but Principal Ryan looked embarrassed or angry or both.

Mrs. Rice, the school secretary, had just come outside – I assume to try to shoo us away – when Rob walked up. He was alone. A couple of kids called out to him, but Rob didn't look over at us. He didn't look scared, just a little tense. But I knew him so well now, so intimately, I could almost feel the jaw muscle flexing under his skin. It was all I could do not shout out to him. To tell him they had evidence. As he approached, both men turned to look at him through the glass, disappointment heavy on their faces.

Rob didn't even glance in our direction but walked smoothly into the office as if nothing was wrong. I just stood there, me and at least twenty other kids, and watched him deny the accusation again as he had the night before. Obviously, I couldn't hear what Rob was saying but I recognized the tilt of his head, the raised eyebrows, the furrowed brow – every expression conveying confidence, innocence, concern. But before Rob had even stopped talking, I saw Mr. Starr's cheeks redden with anger. And it was clear he was shouting. He held up the plastic bag and shook it. When Rob looked confused, Mr. Starr practically tore the bag open and pulled Rob's uniform from inside. He pushed up to Rob's face. Rob stepped back. And then a look of understanding lit his eyes. He'd been caught. Apparently, the smell of gasoline doesn't wash out so easily.

I'm not sure what happened after that. The crowd dispersed when Principal Ryan came out and shouted at everyone. I had no choice but to go home. When I got there, my mother was sitting at the kitchen table going over some bills and seeing her, I suddenly realized what should have occurred to me already. It was her. She had found Rob's uniform in the washing machine. It was she who had ratted Rob out. My throat went dry. How could she have done something so awful? What could she have been thinking? Rob was going to get in serious trouble – maybe even get suspended or get kicked off the team. He was going to hate her, or worse – hate me.

If I'd been expecting an apology or some sign of regret, I couldn't have been more off the mark. When my mother looked up, I knew immediately that she was furious. I had lied to her. I had helped Rob cover up his lie. I had lied to the police. And then she started on other things; things she'd hadn't brought up before; my falling grades, my "questionable" clothing choices. "What the hell was going on?" she shouted. "Someone could have died". "What the hell were Rob and his friends thinking?" "What the hell were you thinking?"

I was grounded for two weeks. Which meant I was going to miss the rest of basketball season. Not that it mattered since Rob probably wouldn't be playing anyway. Oh, and as you've probably already guessed, the Starrs were moving out.

Believe it or not, none of that mattered to me. The only thing I cared about was Rob. I was out of my mind with worry and no way to get any information. I tried to text him, but he wasn't answering. Had his father taken the phone? Had the school confiscated it? Finally, out of desperation, I texted Kendal –not something I normally did but I needed intel. I tried to sound nonchalant and gossipy, and luckily Kendal didn't seem at all surprised to hear from me. I guess when something happens as huge as Rob Starr getting caught nuking a building in another town, all phone lines are open.

Kendal told me that she'd heard from Mike that Rob had gone back to practice until they figured out what to do with him.

She'd also heard that he told the principal that the whole thing was his idea and his fault. Of course, Rob refused to implicate any of his teammates. "Rob would never narc on his friends," she texted. He even got Reynolds out of trouble by telling them he'd made Reynolds wait for him in the car. I texted very little beyond "NFW" and "SO not fair." When we signed off, I sat on my bed and literally prayed that no one would figure out my mother's part in all of it.

Rob didn't get in until much later that night. My mom and dad had been quiet all evening and had gone upstairs early – I'm sure it was to avoid seeing Rob. They did, however, leave a note on the kitchen table telling the boys to pack their stuff – move out day was to be that coming weekend.

I hugged Rob when he came in and he hugged me back to my huge relief. He explained that his father was really mad at first, but he eventually calmed down and "handled shit". From what Rob told me, it sounded like Mr. Starr offered to pay all damages and medical bills and "contribute a major chunk of money" to the school, if Port Windsor agreed to drop the charges. His father also spoke with the Coach and Principal Ryan and they agreed to put Rob on "private suspension" for three days.

In case you're wondering, private suspension isn't a real thing. It was something they'd invented just for Rob. It meant that, although he was getting punished – he wouldn't be able to play in the semi-final – the reason for his absence would not be shared with anyone. The "incident" would not go on his permanent record. In other words, it wouldn't mess up his chances of getting recruited for college ball.

Even at the time, I knew he'd gotten off easy – beyond easy – considering the damage that had been done. But Rob didn't see it that way at all. He was angry. The game he was missing was against one of the best teams in the state. And now – because of those Port Windsor assholes, Ellsworth would have to face them without their best player. "It fucking sucks," he moaned.

I felt bad for Rob. I really did. But I also kind of didn't. I mean it was – I don't know… frustrating, infuriating, exasperating. Why were they letting him get away with it? Why was everything so easy for him? Why did the world work so differently for some people?

Plus, while I didn't want to admit it – particularly to myself – it was kind of disturbing how convincingly Rob had lied. It was almost impossible to tell which parts were true and which were made up. It made me realize that he was probably lying about other stuff too. Like maybe at The Halloween Haunt, it was Rob and his buddies who trashed the parking lot that night. And even way back in October, the night of the bonfire; was it Rob who'd stolen that sixty dollars from my mom's handbag? Was he really just a spoiled douche, like Jake said?

Later that night my mother came downstairs, and before we were aware of her, she walked in on Rob and me sitting close together. I think I might have even had my hand on his thigh. It wasn't sexual or anything, but it was sort of intimate. I quickly moved away from him, but it didn't matter anyway. Our closeness hadn't registered with her. It was obvious by the way she wrung her hands that she had something else on her mind. She cleared he throat a couple of times before she spoke.

"Rob, I can see that you're upset, and I want you to know that I'm sorry about all of this."

Rob looked up at her like he wasn't quite understanding what she was saying. She continued.

"You know how much I care about you boys, and you know I love your mom like a sister." She took a deep breath. "But I felt I had to say something. It was just too serious …and well… too big a thing not to involve your dad."

Rob stared at her blankly and I could tell that, until that moment, he hadn't known it was her. Or maybe he just hadn't thought about it – hadn't considered how his father had found out. He had been too busy thinking about the outcome to consider the source. Then he turned and looked at me. I shook my head vehemently. He couldn't possibly think I was involved.

"Mia didn't tell me, if that's what you're thinking," my mother said (and I could have hugged her for it). This morning when I opened the dryer, I found your basketball uniform in there, stinking of gasoline. And well…"

Just FYI – it turns out you need vinegar and baking soda to wash out the smell of gasoline. It's something you can find out in like, one second, if you search the internet. How could I have let Rob down like that?

Rob said nothing, but his cheeks were red with anger. My mother continued.

"I'm sure you saw my note," she said. "You and Jake will be moving back in with your dad on Saturday morning. And I know you don't believe me right now but this whole thing just breaks my heart. I've loved having you boys here with me." At that point, her voice cracked a little like she was going to cry. "It's just that… I'm not sure I'm doing such a good job." She sniffed. "Perhaps it's best, anyway."

Rob couldn't look her, and he didn't even try to speak. He just nodded.

"Well. Okay then," she said quietly and walked into the kitchen.

Rob sat perfectly still for about five seconds. Then he stood up and walked out of the room.

CHAPTER 34

The End Begins

February 7ᵗʰ

I was startled awake the next morning by Rob standing at the foot of my bed. It was barely dawn, and the sky outside my window was a sort of pinky-brown. I couldn't quite make out Rob's face in the semi-darkness but just the set of his shoulders suggested something was wrong. For a moment, my still-sleepy brain couldn't figure it out what was happening. Did something happen with Mrs. G-S? No...that wasn't it. And then the memory of the past couple of days came back to me like a match catching flame: the gasoline, the uniform, the suspension... and I knew what was coming.

I can remember that morning in almost perfect detail. Maybe it was the cocoon-like quietness of the house, or the soft blanket of winter morning light, but for whatever reason it had an uncanny clarity that sticks to me still. And when I think about that morning – which I try not to do if I can help it – I can recall every awful moment as if it's happening again.

"Hey." Rob says.

"Hey, what time is it?" I ask, my voice filled with sleep

"I don't know. Early. We need to talk," Rob says.

"Okay," I say, yawning. I half wish and half pretend that I don't know what he's talking about. I scoot myself over and push back the covers for him to join me. "What do you want to talk about?" I ask flirtatiously. Rob hesitates then sits on the edge of the bed. I can see that he's struggling to say something. I know what it is, but I ask anyway.

"What's wrong?" My heart is in my throat and my breath is thin. *Please don't*, I think. *Please don't break up with me. I love you. Oh my God. Please...I don't care what you did... I forgive you...I'll always forgive you.*

"Nothing." Rob says shaking his head. "It's just...now that we're *finally* moving out..." He emphasizes the word 'finally' as if he's been waiting for this day forever. "I think ...you know... things... have been weird...everything is like totally fucked. Nothing is how it's supposed to be. My mom...and it's been really bad with my dad... and my grades...and the team...the team is really...I don't know if we're gonna win tonight." He sighs and looks past me.

"What do you mean?" I can barely get the words out, but I'm not confused. I know what he's saying. He's saying we're cursed – that everything is going wrong and it's because of us... because of me.

"Of course, we're going to win!" I say emphatically – deliberately ignoring the rest.

I grab his hand, but his fingers are limp in mine. "I'm sorry Mia," he says.

"Sorry?"

"It's just...you know...we're not..."

"Hey," I interrupt, pulling myself out of the covers to crawl closer to him. My pulse is drumming in my ears. I shake his arm to make him look at me. My eyes search his. "You know your mom is

doing so much better. She can call you by name now. And you heard
the doctor say that it was real progress. And don't worry about your
grades, we can get your grades up." I lean in and kiss him on the
neck behind his earlobe. "I'll help you," I whisper. "We can study for
real... and the team...well, the team is going to win tonight. I know
it." I can hear the desperation in my voice, but I can't stop myself.

Rob shrugs. "I just want everything...I need everything to be
normal again."

I slide closer to him. "It is normal," I say. I lean forward and
start kissing him... touching him.

"C'mon, Mia...stop...", he says. But I don't stop. Because I
know I have to save us. And eventually it works – his body re-
sponds – he gives into me. I make him give in to me.

We have sex, but it isn't right. It's mechanical and the opposite
of intimate. He finishes quickly and when he's done, he pulls away.
"You...we shouldn't have..."

"Hey, stop it," I say with false cheerfulness. "Your just upset
and worried about the team and everything. When the team wins
tonight, you'll feel better about everything."

He looks and me and smiles sadly. "Yeah. Sure. Maybe you're
right."

"Totally," I say. But I feel like I've been shot and I'm slowly
bleeding out.

Mr. Starr arrived around ten that morning. He and my father
spoke briefly as they loaded the car. My mother busied herself in
the kitchen – avoiding both Mr. Starr and the boys. When they were
ready to go, Rob thanked my parents stiffly and shook my father's
hand. Then Rob hugged Rachel and told her to be good – she was
staying – of course. My mother hugged Jake and squeezed Rob's
shoulder, but he looked away. There were tears in her eyes as she
watched them head to the car.

You might be thinking that I was in my room bawling my eyes out. But I wasn't. I didn't cry because I wasn't sad. I was sick. A ball of fire was churning in my chest.

Whether I wanted to admit it or not, I could now see how much I'd been using our living arrangement, and by that, I mean sex, to keep Rob interested in me. My behavior earlier that morning was the ugly proof.

And the brutal lesson I was learning that day was that sex doesn't fix anything; it doesn't save anything. In fact, it can make things worse. I realized that no one had ever told me how bad it could make me feel. No one ever told me that having sex with someone could be heartbreaking, lonely, desperate, and completely humiliating.

And now I was faced with the question that if Rob couldn't have sex with me, would he still want me? And I think we all already know the answer to that one.

But then, surprisingly, as I predicted, the team won that night and Rob called me after the game. His voice was a loud whisper under a cupped hand, but I could still hear everyone going crazy in the background. "Hey! Can you hear me? We won! You were right! You were right!" I started to answer but it was too loud, and he was too distracted to hear me. "I'm coming!" he shouted to someone in the background.

"That's what she said," I said automatically.

"Gotta go," he said loudly into the phone.

"Sure, okay," I said. "See you...I'm mean, I'll text you later."

"Yup...okay," He answered but he was no longer listening.

CHAPTER 35

Seasons End

February 21ˢᵗ

W eeks went by and Rob and I barely saw each other. He'd cancelled our Trig sessions to spend more time at basketball practice. When we passed in the hall at school, he acted like he always had – like we were friends – that was it. He seemed distracted but generally fine. I, on the other hand, was a desperately, quietly, freaking out. I had no idea what he was thinking. Could I call him? How were we going to see each other? I tried texting him, but his answers were short and delayed. Why hadn't we worked this stuff out before he moved out? And of course, there was the upcoming game to consider. Maybe life was just on hold until then. Maybe we'd work all this stuff out afterwards. It wasn't fair to bother him when he had so much on his mind – right? And maybe if they won, Rob would relax, and we could be a couple like he said…like he promised.

Finally, many empty, confusing days later, the Saturday night of the basketball final finally arrived. Things seemed hopeful. The team had worked hard to get there – Rob most of all. He'd given just about everything to the season. The opposing team – the

Hawks – were the best in the division, but we'd beat them once before in the regular season so there really was a chance. Plus, we had home court advantage.

Rob had texted me the night before to be sure I was coming to the game. Even though we hadn't spoken much, he seemed anxious to have me there, maybe because his mother wouldn't be. My parents, thank God, gave me the night off from being grounded because it was a special occasion.

The game was exciting. The Eagles were playing well and Rob seemed calm and in control. He even hit two three-point shots in the first period. And I could see from his body language that the better they played the more Rob relaxed. By halfway through the second period he was acting as though nothing had changed between us. He looked over at me before every free throw and once he even winked. I'd nod the way I always did, and he'd hit it – every time. Anyway, that's how it went for most of the game.

The Eagles were up by two as the clock ticked down on the last period, but the Hawks fought back hard, and the game went into overtime. Still, I believed Rob had this. He knew how to win. He forced a foul on a tall, baby-faced forward whose emotions had been running too hot the whole game. It was almost too easy. And Rob was awarded two shots. He stood at the free throw line and went through the motions. Everything was as it should be – the sound of the crowd pounding their feet, two bounces, the glance at me, the nod back to him, another bounce and then, the ball dropped through the basket – all net. Everyone went crazy – we were one up and he still had another shot coming. Rob waited a few seconds for the crowd to quiet but no one could contain themselves – we were all on our feet. He bounced the ball twice. He looked at me. I was holding my breath. I think I was more nervous than he was. I nodded, and Rob bounced the ball a third time. He shot – and missed.

The ball bounced off the rim and into the hands of a tall bruiser of a guy who was down the court in a few loping strides.

I know it seems impossible, but I swear, at that moment, all the sound stopped. And while everyone else was turned towards the action, my eyes never left Rob. He was motionless – stunned – his shock overriding his well-trained basketball instinct to move. And I could tell by his expression that he knew it was over. He'd lost the game and something more. His eyes flicked over to me but before I could react, he was off – down the court – shouting for the ball.

The bruiser – a point guard – was more height than skill. He missed the layup but got his own rebound. He passed the ball back to their star player, a bird-like black kid named Ronnie, who – based on the heartfelt "Ron-E Ron-E Ron-E" coming from the other side of the gym – was adored by his fans as much as Rob was by us. He went for the 3-pointer and hit it. My eyes traveled over the cheering Hawk fans across the court. Which one of those girls was Ronnie's, I wondered? A second later the buzzer sounded. Out of time. Game over.

So, before I go any further, I want you to know that I'm still me. Even though it may not seem that way – hell, I barely recognize myself in all this. But I promise, I'm still the same awkward, snarky, art club, mathlete who's become the phony, friendless, fake basketball groupie you've come this far with. But what I did this night or almost did, will make you think differently. So, I'm telling you now, that I'm still the same. Okay maybe I'm not exactly the same. But I'm different *because* of what happened not the other way around.

The next hour was a blur. I stood with the cheerleaders and the fans and the other players – as near to Rob as I could get – and watched the blizzard of handshakes and back pats and "good-games" and "we'll-get'em-next-years". Then there was a wave of logistics – who was going where and how and with who.

Eventually it was agreed that we, the kids, would still go over to the Reynolds house for the afterparty even though we didn't win and even though there was a probably a big Congratulations banner stretched across the living room wall. At one point Casey grabbed my arm and said, "You're definitely coming to Reynold's, right?" I nodded, grateful that someone had noticed I was there. The stands emptied out and families peeled away. Most of the team had already headed into the locker room to shower and change before I finally dared to approach Rob. "Oh…hey," he said, the disappointment heavy in his voice.

"So, I'll see you later… at the party?" I said quickly as if I suddenly had somewhere to be.

"Yeah, sure," he said blankly.

I walked from the school to my house by myself. I remember the drumming of my heart in my ears and the feeling of dread. It was as if I could physically feel Rob slipping away from me and the panic was inching up the back of my throat practically strangling me. I couldn't let that happen. I had no ride and no one to go with, but I knew I had to get to that party. I had to fix things. I had to be there.

In a little less than an hour, wearing what I thought was one of my best party outfits (tight black jeans and tiny cropped t-shirt with buttons down the front). I asked my mom to drive me to the Prince's. She hesitantly agreed, but not before asking a bunch of questions like who was going to be there and what would be served, all of which I anticipated and deflected. On the way over she asked me more than once if I was okay. I looked at her like she was crazy. "You mean besides the fact that we lost?" I said hostilely. She sighed. When she pulled up to the house she said, "You know I don't like these kids."

I shrugged. "Everyone is going to be here. Not just *these* kids."

"Are Stephanie and Carmen going to be there?"

"Pretty much everyone," I said again. Of course, they weren't invited, but it was still hard to lie to her flat out.

The Princes lived in a one of the mcmansions over by the golf course. The house was designed to look like a small castle. I rang the doorbell, but no one answered. I could hear the party through the thick leaded windows that flanked the massive front door. I rang the bell again. I was a little uncomfortable just letting myself in, but my mother was still sitting in the car and I knew she wouldn't leave till I was safely inside. I went for the doorknob but suddenly the door swung open and I was face to face with the handsome and always flirty Mike Egan. A wave of smoke and music greeted me before he did.

"Welcome Little b!" he said too loudly. "Aren't you a sight for sore...whatever?..." He waggled his eyebrows comically.

"Hi Mike, sorry about the game," I said politely. This had become a thing with Rob's friends. They acted like horny idiots and I acted like I didn't notice.

I stepped into the foyer, which was bigger than our living room. It was white stucco with dark wood – more of the middle-ages castle look – complete with a large curving staircase and two arched doorways– one to the dining room, one to a hallway that probably led to the kitchen. To the left and down three or four stairs was the living room which was the size of a small gymnasium. It was crowded, which meant there must have been about a hundred kids there already.

"No worries. We've got plenty of spike, lots of weed and we're shit out of parents – so it's all good."

"Great...um, have you seen Rob?"

Mike glanced over his shoulder vaguely. "In here somewhere but you can't come in unless you do a shot – those are Reynolds house rules." He gestured to a small table by the door set up with a several bottles of tequila, shot glasses, a bowl of cut limes and a shaker of salt.

"Yeah sure…but, no thanks," I said. "I'm just going to find Rob. I, uh, need to tell him something." I tried to move past Mike, towards the stairs but he quickly blocked my way.

"What's the deal?" I said, trying to step around him.

"Rules are rules," he said. "Everyone has to do a shot to make up for the shot we missed. That's what it takes to get in."

"Fine…whatever."

Mike grinned with victory. "I'll bet you've never done one of these…"

As Mike demonstrated the proper procedure of doing a tequila shot – which included a fairly disgusting ritual of 1) licking and salting part of your hand 2) then licking the salt off your hand, 3) doing a shot of tequila – which is full-on make-you-gag horrific by the way – and 4) sucking on a lime – as if that somehow made up for swallowing something that tasted like flaming vomit. I kept trying to get a glimpse of Rob's light brown hair. He had to be in there somewhere.

Looking back now, I can honestly say that I already knew something wasn't right – I mean, besides the fact that we'd lost the game and that things between Rob and me were weird. There was something harder and louder about the party – an angry energy in the air. And there were other clues. Like Rob. He was usually in the center of things with Mike and Justin right beside him so, where was he? And why was Mike so amped up – so insistent that I do a shot – he'd never cared if I drank or not before?

"Whoo!" Mike shouted as he slammed his shot glass on the table. "Awesome, right?"

I nodded. I hadn't eaten anything for a while and the tequila was burning in my throat and stomach. "Now can I go in?" I asked.

"Be Reynolds' guest," Mike said, gesturing grandly.

I made my way down the three steps into the living room and pushed myself into the crowd. Everyone was already well on their way to getting wasted. I guess losing is an even better reason to get drunk than winning. Without Rob to stand next to, I didn't really have an anchor, so I sort of aimlessly wove my way through the room hoping to bump into him. Instead, I ran into Kendal. She was still in her cheer uniform and had a large yellow cup in her hand with something red in it which she nearly spilled on me when she threw her arm around my shoulder. Her face was too close to mine and I could see that her heavy, "game-ready" makeup was smudged. Discernable tear tracks had carved their way through her blush and there was a ball of mascara in the corner of one eye. "Isn't this just the worst?" she said, her lips only inches from my face. Her breath smelled like cherry cough syrup on steroids. I nodded. "And of course, Justin's being a total dick – as if it's my fault we lost or something." It took me a second to register what she meant. But then I remembered that the two of them had been hooking up lately. I nodded again and tried to look sympathetic.

"You need a drink!" Kendal said suddenly, her practiced cheer-leader enthusiasm snapping on like a light bulb. She dragged me sideways through the crowd, her arm still wrapped around my neck. We made our way to a marble-topped serving table which held a large glass punch bowl. I was handed my very own yellow cup. "To the best team in the world" Kendal said weepily, and we bumped our plastic glasses together and drank. The punch was sweet and not entirely unpleasant. I took a few gulps and looked around for Rob.

An argument broke out across the makeshift dancefloor and Kendal headed over to investigate. She gestured for me to follow but as soon as she was deep enough in the crowd I turned and headed back towards the kitchen, guessing Rob would be there. He wasn't. Reynolds was in the center of things, a couple of adoring sophomores fluttering around him like butterflies. He saw me. I'm pretty sure of it. But he looked away before I could be certain. I took another large swallow of my drink and realized, to my surprise that my cup was empty. I headed back towards the living room for a refill. Why not? I thought. I mean it didn't taste like it had much alcohol in it and it was certainly better than the tequila.

On my way back through the foyer, I found Mike back at his welcome station instructing two JV ballers on the art of the tequila shot. "Hey beautiful, ready for another one?" He called out as I passed.

I wasn't going to do the shot. The first one tasted horrible. But I was already a little drunk – okay more than a little – and I was starting to get annoyed with Rob. It wasn't just because he was nowhere to be found but because of everything – the way he'd been ignoring me since he'd moved out – the way he made me feel guilty that he'd missed the shot – as if I'd let him down – as if everything bad that happened to him was somehow my fault. And Mike was being flirty but in nicer way than usual. So, when he held out the saltshaker, I dutifully stuck my hand out to be seasoned. As I licked the salt off my skin I looked up towards the stairs. I don't know why I looked that way. Maybe it was fate or maybe it was intuition, but there they were on the landing – Rob and Chloe. They were standing almost toe to toe, his tall, lean body arcing over her tiny, perfect form. She had two fingers hooked into the front right pocket of his jeans, and she was leaning back a little, using him for balance as she stared up into his face.

They weren't kissing but they would be soon. Anybody looking at them could tell.

I'm pretty sure Mike saw me see them. But when I turned my eyes back to him, he just handed me a shot and held his up for me to toast.

"To the sexiest girl at the party," he said looking into my eyes. I felt as if I were suffocating. I took a quick, sharp breath in and then another but still couldn't get any air. Everything seemed to be moving both too slowly and too fast. My chest was constricting with pain, humiliation, anger. We stood there for a second, me and Mike, both of us wondering what would happen next – could I take the punch or was I going down?

I reached out and steadied myself with the edge of the table and forced myself to breathe. Then I nodded once and touched my cup to his. "Go Eagles," I said.

He laughed. "To the fuckin' Eagles!" he shouted into the living room and a handful of bystanders cheered with him. We drank. The shot was bigger than the first one, but the burning sensation wasn't as bad the second time around.

"Easy there, tiger," Mike said as I tipped a little on the heel of my boot.

"Strong stuff," I said with a small laugh as if it were the shot that had knocked me off balance.

"Here, suck on this," Mike said handing me a lime wedge, eyebrows raised. I smiled vaguely at his innuendo, but I was no longer looking at him. I was looking past him to the staircase. No one was there.

CHAPTER 36

Say "Cheese"

February 21ˢᵗ continued

After I obediently sucked on the lime wedge, I picked up my yellow cup and turned to head back into the party. There was really no other choice. Where else could I go? I had no friends there – no ride home. I couldn't call my parents – they would freak if they saw me like this. They'd probably have the whole party shut down.

"Don't go far," Mike called out after me, but the music was so loud it was easy to pretend I hadn't heard him.

I'd never really been drunk before. I mean *really* drunk. And if I'm sticking with my honesty thing, I have to admit, some part of me kind of liked it. Or maybe I was grateful for it. The blunt, buzzy feeling of the alcohol and the loud thumping of the music turned the miserable ache in my stomach into a sort of adrenalized energy. I remember thinking, there should be a word for this feeling, a phrase – like pain power or hate fuel. My brain was spinning with loosely connected thoughts; fuck Rob… Mr. Robbie, Rob, Ringo Rock Starr. I was tired of chasing him around anyway. I was sick of worrying if I was doing the right thing all the time. He wasn't so perfect. He was a fricking *criminal* for fuck's sake (apparently, I swore a lot more when I was drunk). Maybe he hadn't noticed but I was HOT. Guys were into me. Cute guys like Mike Eagan, and some others too. And I bet if I wanted to, Mike would mack with me right now. Oh, and I love this song...

This was about the time that everything changed. I felt weird, woozy. Everything got hazy and I started to lose the linear flow of time. Here's what I remember:

Kendal and some other Baditudes are dancing. I move through the crowd to dance with them – not worrying (maybe for the first time) if they want me there or not. Of course they do. They're my friends. Right?

We dance – or more like bump into people and laugh. We sing along to the song at the top of our lungs – and then the next song which we also LOVE. Then Reynolds appears with shots of something brown in plastic cups. I poured one into another and drink it in one gulp. Wooooohoooo! There are about a million people in Reynold's living room. Someone knocks over a lamp – it crashes on the floor and everyone cheers. And WHERE THE FUCK IS ROB? With Chloe, I remember, probably making out, but *like* who *like* even *like* fucking cares!!!!!!!

Another shot and a few songs later. Kendal and I are dancing for the boys, I think it was some old song and we're singing and sort of rubbing against each other. And the boys are chanting "Kiss, Kiss, Kiss" and I think she is even going to really kiss me on the mouth, but I turn away. About that same time, someone grabs me. And for a second, I think it's Rob. It's Mike. Then we're dancing – more like grinding – and I'm trying to be into it but I'm losing a little steam. Where is Rob anyway? Then I think I see him, and I push closer to Mike. But then I think it might have been Jake. That judge-y face. Who does he think he is anyway? Always gawking at me and Rob with that mopey, kicked-puppy look.

Mike and I do another shot. I have the hiccups. He tells me he has the perfect cure – wants to show me something so cool. Something in Reynolds house. I follow him. He has me by the hand, but I stumble a little. And then we're in this huge, dark room with a pool. An indoor pool. Shit, the Princes are rich. This strikes me as funny. "The Princes are rich," I say, laughing. "Of course they are – they're princes!" Then Mike and I are making out but it's not good. His tongue is too big and gaggy and he's breathing too hard and his hands are all over me. He tries to take off my shirt. "Stop," I say, and he laughs at me. "We're just going swimming. It'll be fun. Get rid of your hiccups." Then Kendal and Justin show up with a bottle of tequila. And then Kendal's not wearing a top. She lets Justin do a "body shot" of tequila off her bare chest. Then it's Mike's turn. He's licking Kendal's chest and she's pushing him away but not really. I feel weird. Like I'm supposed to think it's normal to do that stuff in front of people, but I don't.

Kendal tries to hand me a yellow cup. I don't remember her having it before. I shake my head. I don't feel so great. "This will make you feel better," she says.

"You gave her two?" Justin asks.

"Shut up Justin," Kendal says. "She doesn't feel well – she needs two."

I take a big gulp. It's punch. It doesn't make me feel better.

Kendal makes us pose for a group selfie.

I think Kendal and Justin are somewhere macking, but I don't remember them leaving. Then they're back and taking more pictures. I'm starting to miss things – chunks of time – blanks. I see things in snapshots like an old movie with some of the frames burned out. Mike's too-big tongue in my mouth. Kendal's purple-thonged butt popping up from the water as she demonstrates a summersault. Justin, naked, diving off the diving board. Mike pulling the leg of my jeans over my foot. Us in the water. My wet under-wear clinging to my skin. More pictures. Mike kissing me – push-ing me up against the rough cement side of the pool – pulling at my bra.

Justin is there. "C'mon, let's see little b," he says. "Shut up," I say. I'm confused. How does he know what Little b means? I try to hit him and slip. I go under the water and he holds my head down near his crotch. Then he lets me up. I gasp. They laugh. My wet hair is in my mouth. I feel ill.

"Get away from me," I say. I push at Justin, but he is much stronger and heavier than me. He's crushing me. I feel like I'm suffocating.

Finally, I manage to speak. "I'm going to be sick," I say but Justin doesn't get it. I hear Kendal's voice from somewhere behind me. "Say cheese!"

Then I'm sick. I think I throw up on Justin and in the pool. Justin is swearing. He calls me a disgusting bitch and then laughs, and I don't know what after that. I'm sick again. At some point, someone pulls me out of the water. I feel my stomach scraping the side. I hear snippets of the conversation. "Can't just leave her here." I'm in a pool chair, hands pulling at my clothes and hair. More laughing. "She's fine – we're done here anyway." "What did I do with my bag?" "Smile Mia!"

I must pass out because when I come to again it's quiet. They're gone. There's a puddle of vomit and a vomit-y pool towel beside me. I am mostly undressed. Panties on but soaked and see-thru, bra on, but open – it's the kind that opens in the front. I am wet. My hair is stuck on my face and neck. I push it away and realize it's caked with throw up.

I feel desperately around for my clothes. I honestly believe I can get myself together. But I can't seem to work my bra. I try several times but looking down at the clasp makes me feel like I'm going to throw up. I see my shirt on another chair but it's hard to get there. The ground is spinning. I lurch and fall. My forehead hits the ground hard. Blood on my fingers. Somehow, I get to my shirt. I sit on the ground and put it on, backwards but I'm too tired to try again. My jeans are in a pink puddle of punch and water. I wrap the dirty towel around my waist and drag my pants to the side of the pool. I try to rinse out my jeans and then my hair without falling in, but I have to move very slowly, or I'll throw up again. I hear voices. I think its Rob. For a second, I want to shout out to him to help me but then I remember. The voices are louder. I consider hiding but can't move. Then Reynolds and Candie there – laughing, flirting. They stop when they see me.

Reynolds: "What the hell…?"

Me: "Wassith Mike." I'm not speaking clearly.

"Fuckin' Mike," Reynolds says rubbing his hand over the back of his tightly cropped hair. "He was supposed to handle this. Do you know what time it is? Look at this place – my parents are going to lose it." He looks around as if Mike might somehow appear from the shadows with a mop.

Candie: "Okay. Okay…We got to get her out of here. Do you think we should call Rob?"

I can't hear what Reynolds says in reply. Then he says, "Just stay with her. I'll be back."

If I expected sympathy or help from Candie, none comes. I manage to ask her if she has seen Rob – my words as slow and slurred. She says "Whaddayoucare? You were with Mike and half the other guys at the party."

I consider protesting but I don't have the energy. If I move or talk, I'll throw up again for sure. We sit in silence waiting for someone, but I can't remember who. It takes a long time. Candie plays a game on her phone. I concentrate on not moving and not throwing up. I think I pass out again. Then Reynolds is back, and Rob is with him. I start to cry. "I'm so sorry," I say.

"C'mon Mia. We've got to go."

"I dun have anypans on," I manage. I feel drugged and nauseated and humiliated and disgusting.

Reynolds: "Just take the towel and get her out of here."

"Thanks man," Rob says, "we'll bring it back." He sounds funny. Weird. Mad, maybe?

"Don't. And don't bring her back either," Reynolds says. Candie laughs falsely.

We get outside through the kitchen door. Rob is half carrying me as I can't seem to get my legs to work right. I keep telling him I'm sorry, but he doesn't say anything. I'm trying to hold the towel around me and I'm clinging to my wet jeans as if my life somehow depends on getting them safely out of the Prince household. The cold air feels good on my face, but I suddenly realize I have no shoes on. I can't remember what shoes I was wearing. Boots? I say something about my boots, but Rob tells me not to worry about it. We'll get them tomorrow. Why is he being so nice? He loves Chloe, not me. The thought hits me like a train. I have to stop and vomit on the front lawn.

I lay face down on the grass. I don't want to be with Rob. I want to die.

Rob tries to get me to get up. "Fuck you," I shout into the ground. Finally, he picks me up and throws me over his shoulder. He carries me to the car and puts me in the back. "Don't throw up," he says. His voice sounds different. Whose car are we in? The drive is only a few minutes, but I fall asleep, or pass out, which is probably more accurate.

I'm not sure how we get from the car to the front door. I am sitting down on the step when the door swings open. My father looks down at me. His face is white with worry. Rob is already gone.

CHAPTER 37

Misery

February 22nd

The next day was miserable. I was sicker than I've ever been in my life. And to make things worse, my parents weren't even mad. Sure, that sounds like something I should have been grateful for, but it actually sucked. You see, instead of being mad, they were scared and freaked and seriously disappointed which, for the record, is way worse than mad. The concern in their faces was frightening – my father's especially – probably because he'd witnessed his eldest daughter – a child he'd often referred to as "his sunny sunshine" – half naked and puking on the oriental rug in the front hall. He kept looking at me as if he'd never seen me before. And there was this sadness in his eyes – the look of someone who'd witnessed a tragedy.

I told them repeatedly that I didn't know what had happened. I said I didn't know how I got home. I said I thought it was some of the girls from the party.

When my parents asked me if Rob or Jake were involved and I said "no". But really, I wanted to scream YES. Yes, Rob was involved. He was the cause of the whole thing. He was the reason for everything I did, or thought, or was. But I didn't say any of that. Because even then, I felt the need to protect him – us.

They grounded me for the "foreseeable future", which I didn't really care that much about but when they took my phone away, I basically lost it. I cried hysterically. I begged them not to. What if Rob was trying to text me or call me?

I spent the whole day in bed and the bathroom, and all the time convinced that Rob was trying to reach me – texting me to see if I was okay. I was so deep into my crazy rationalization I even managed to excuse his behavior with Chloe. I mean so what if he had been hanging with her? They were friends. Sure, they seemed kind of cozy on the stairs, but I was drunk – or at least on my way to being drunk – maybe I had misinterpreted it.

Besides, you can't just stop loving someone – just like that, can you? That's just not how it works. And he did eventually come and find me. He did drive me home and made sure I was safe. Right?

But every hour that went by I got a little bit less hungover and my thoughts got a little clearer and it got a lot harder to deny what was really happening. I knew the truth. I'd known for a while. I knew the morning he showed up in my room and maybe even before that. Maybe even back when I saw Chloe at the rehab center. And there was certainly no denying the look on his face when that second foul shot bounced off the rim. I saw it in his eyes before he took off down the court – everything he'd been thinking about confirmed – that I was bad luck and that he needed to get things "back to normal" – as if all the time we'd been together and everything that had happened between us was some kind aberration, a virus he'd caught and needed to shake.

Because I had no access to my phone, all of Sunday went by without me knowing the other stuff that was going on but I'm guessing you've already figured it out. Those videos and pictures Kendal had been taking all night – the ones that she pretended to be taking of all of us – well, they were all of me. And they were posted everywhere. The first was around ten in the morning. It was me in my bra and jeans, chugging rum out of the bottle. The next was posted an hour or so later – a picture of me passed out, topless with vomit on my mismatched boobs and in my hair. Some photo app had been used to scrawl the words *little b* over the smaller side of my meager chest. And the posts got worse as the day went on. New videos going up every couple of hours – a gif of Mike pushing up against me from behind, his face conveniently out of the frame, another of me coming up out of the water right in front of a naked Justin McCoud (also unidentifiable) – spitting and sputtering as if I'd just …well you get it.

The truth? It happened. I won't deny it now and I didn't then. *Some* of it happened. I did kiss Mike Egan and maybe Justin too. And yes, Mike pushed me into wall of the pool from behind, but we didn't have sex and I pushed him off me seconds later. And I admit I'd been under water in front of Justin naked body but only because he shoved me under and kept me down there until I almost drowned.

The whole thing had been a set up – Kendal, Mike, and Justin and Candie too probably and probably the rest of the Baditudes. All orchestrated by the one and only Chloe Olsen.

So, the 'Idiot of the Century Award' goes to (drumroll please) …Mia Morgan. And I think we can all agree, I deserved it. I mean, I knew what was happening all along, didn't I? I'd been pretending for weeks, maybe even months, that these girls really liked me – ignoring every warning sign. Because I wanted to. Because so would you – so would everyone – everyone like me anyway, every insecure high school nobody with frizzy hair and an oily t-zone who'd ever wished or fantasized that someday they'd be noticed, that they would matter.

And lucky me; now I did. I mattered in the way that no one should ever matter. I was *that* girl. The poor, pathetic soul you hear about in your high school or maybe the high school a couple of towns over from yours. You know, the one who was passed out while having a "threesome" with some guys at a party, or the video you saw of some girl giving some manipulative asshole a blowjob because he said he really liked her. Well, that was me. And my life was basically over. Oh sure, the school insisted that everyone take the pictures down. They threatened that anyone who posted them would be severely punished, but by the time that happened the damage was long since done – saved in the photo libraries of half the students in the Senior Class.

By the time I convinced my parents to give me my phone back (4 days later), not just the other kids had seen it but everyone; teachers, administrators, parents, *my* parents. I stayed out of school for a couple of days but ultimately, I had to go. The only other option would have been private school and it was just too late in the school year to make the change. Not that it would have made a difference. My story would have followed me in a matter of days.

That first day back I walked down the halls barely breathing – a burning empty feeling where my guts should have been. The boys hooted. The girls laughed. No one talked to me. Not even the teachers acknowledged me.

Later that day I saw Rob and Chloe in the hall by the gym. They were next to each other in a crowd of Baditudes and Basketballers – they were so close together they were touching – her shoulder pressing against his arm. He didn't see me at first, but she did. "Hey Mia," she called out loudly. "Coming to the barty this weekend?" The whole group turned and looked at me. A few people laughed, but it was fake, nervous.

"I swear, there is something seriously wrong with you," Rob said to her, shaking his head. But his tone was affectionate, as if he were scolding a mischievous child.

Time slowed down. My heart pounded in my ears and my breath left me.

I resisted glancing back at Rob until I was almost at the end of the hall. To my surprise he was watching me. And there was something in the turn of his mouth. Sadness? Pity? Whatever it was, it was almost too horrible to bear. I ran to the nearest girl's room and barely got the door of the stall closed before I started to cry.

I now knew why kids killed themselves over bullying. No kidding. I wanted to die. It felt like I was drowning; drowning under layers and layers of humiliation – my drunken, hideous face, my freakish breasts, the sex acts I didn't commit, the fool-ishness of thinking Rob really cared about me, and the fact that these girls who I stupidly convinced myself might actually like me had purposely set out to ruin my life. It was all too much to bear.

After about a minute, I heard the door open and close. Had someone come in after me? I held my breath. For a split second, I thought maybe it was Rob. Pathetic – I know. But for a moment I let myself think maybe…maybe it was all somehow salvageable. Maybe if he knew that none of it was real, that I thought those boys were gross, that it was all a set up designed to break us up – maybe then he'd be mad at them for hurting me. He'd forgive me. He'd take me back.

It wasn't Rob. Whoever it was went into another stall and shut the door. I took the opportunity to come out of mine and splash some water on my face. But when I looked up Kendal was stand-ing behind me. Our reflections stared at each other for a several seconds until finally she said, "Don't look at me like that, bitch. You brought this on yourself."

I must have shaken my head because she said "What? You don't remember? You don't recall that you've been lying to us for the last four months? You were fucking Chloe's boyfriend for the last four months and you can't remember it? Or you just didn't think we'd figure it out?

How did she… how could they…? I tried to talk but I wasn't sure what to say. "I wasn't…we…"

"Don't," she said putting up her hand. "Don't even fucking start lying again. We've known about everything ever since Chloe got that text from Rob that was obviously meant for you."

I shook my head again. What? And then my memory clicked into place. The text I never got after the Halloween Haunt. Turned out Rob had been telling the truth. He had sent a text – just not to me.

"We didn't mean to hurt anyone," I said quietly.

She laughed. "We? What we? Are you kidding me? Rob was only with you for the sex. He fucks around on Chloe every time they get into one of their fights. Why do you think she convinced you to do it with him? So, he could just be done with you and move on."

With that she walked out of the bathroom.

CHAPTER 38

The Lowest Point

March 6th

S o, if you think that was bad, well, buckle up because it gets worse. The next two weeks were total torture. Literally. I was literally being tortured. SLUT was written across my locker in nail polish. I was called slut to my face so many times it didn't even register after a while. When I wore my Baditude clothes, I got mocked for dressing "like the little slut I was". And if I wore my "invisible" clothes the Baditudes called me "faker" or "loser" or "little gay boy" – which just shows you how unevolved they were. And when they got bored of those, they moved on to my lopsided chest – "one tit wonder", "circus freak" and my personal favorite "dwarf boob". For the record, my boobs weren't that different from one another – like a half cup size – but it didn't matter. They could tell it bothered me, so they used it. Isn't that the definition of torture? Finding a vulnerability and poking at it until the person breaks? The harassment at lunch and after school had gotten so bad that my mother came and met me at noon every day – bringing me a sandwich to eat in the car and then picking me up again when the day was over. I hadn't slept, barely ate and my skin was a disaster. As much as my mom was angry at me, I could tell she was also worried.

The following Friday night, my parents went out for dinner and a movie. I should pause here to say that things weren't exactly normal for them either. They were now the "bad parents" of the slutty, drunk girl on the internet. Of course, I tried to explain to them (in embarrassing detail) how the pictures were fakes and how I'd been set up. But since I had to leave all the Rob parts out, they were confused. Why would those kids target me, they wondered? And I had no good answer. Even if they did believe me – which I really hoped they did – what could they do with that information? It's not like they could say to people at a cocktail party, "You know that picture on the internet where it looks like Mia's giving Justin McCloud head? Well, that didn't really happen".

That same night, Hallie and Rachel also had plans – some birthday party fashion show thing, which meant I was home alone. This was not a good for me. I was barely managing to keep it together with other people around. I was lonely, tired, and desperate. Not a good combination. So, against all my better judgement, and everything I knew to be stupid and wrong, I found myself texting Rob. I know…I know…and just when you thought I might have actually learned something.

Me: Hi, I know it's been a while and by now I hope that you have figured out that I didn't do half the stuff in those pictures. It was a total set up. I know how it all looks and I'm so sorry about everything.

No answer.

Me: And I really miss you.

I waited eight minutes. I was going for ten, but couldn't control the ORD.

Me: I know you and Chloe are back together or whatever, but I just want you to know that I still love you and I wish none of this ever happened.

No answer.

Me: And I would give anything if we could just go back to being us.

Me: Rob, I know you care about me. I know you do. I know you must still love me at least a little. If you didn't, you wouldn't have saved me that night. You wouldn't have made sure I was okay. And you know how much I care about you. You are the only thing in the world I really care about.

Five minutes – no answer.

Me: You are just the most amazing person I've ever met, and I can't believe I messed it up by doing all that stupid stuff and I am SO SORRY. PLEASE answer me.

I know. It's mortifying. It makes me queasy even now.

NO. ANSWER.

Me: Please Rob.

Me: I'm so sorry.

Me: PLEASE answer me.

Me: Rob? Please answer me.

Me: Please Rob!!!!!!!!!!!!!!!!!

Four minutes later.

Rob: Please stop texting me.

Me: Please forgive me Rob. I am so sorry. Please give me another chance.

Rob: You have to stop. You are just making it worse for yourself. It's over.

Me: No Rob, you don't mean that. You think you do but you don't. Chloe doesn't care about you like I do.

Nothing.

Me: Please Rob.

Then…

Rob: Stop texting my boyfriend BITCH.

Not Rob. Chloe.

Chloe: He NEVER loved you.

Chloe: Nobody loves a lying slut.

Nausea crept over me like a slow, clammy fog. I imagined Chloe and Rob snuggled together in her pink, fluffy bed. I imagined her grabbing Rob's phone and reading the texts and laughing at how pathetic and desperate I was – her tiny, ragged thumbs punching gleefully at the keys.

I don't know how long I cried after that, but it went on so long that my brain started folding in on itself – like even though I was still crying, I was also sort of watching myself cry and thinking about how crying is really weird. When no one can hear you cry, why do it? What's the point? Maybe it's just a physical reaction so you don't explode. Or is it just a way of exhausting yourself so you can finally turn your brain off? I did finally fall asleep because the next morning my dad woke me up. Our house had been egged. There was egg everywhere, on the windows, in the gutters, all over both our cars. It was awful. We spent most of the afternoon cleaning it up.

At about four thirty, when my dad and I had just finished hosing off the cars for the second time, a BMW pulled up in front of the house. I recognized the car instantly. From where I was standing in our driveway it looked like Rob was driving. My heart nearly stopped. What was he doing here? Was he here about my texts? My hand automatically moved to my frizzy, Saturday hair. It was absurd. As if smoothing down my hair might make some difference at this point. A laugh caught in my throat – the hysterical kind that you do instead of crying – but I managed to contain myself.

My father started across the lawn, when the passenger side door opened and Jake got out. He walked around the car and opened the back door. Mrs. Gerber-Starr slowly stepped out onto the sidewalk. I was shocked. The last time I'd seen her she'd been doing well but I had no idea she was well enough to be released from the treatment center. I did the math in my head. It had been nearly six weeks since my last visit. She looked remarkably well – almost like her old self. Her haired was freshly blonde and her makeup and nails were once again perfection. But when I got closer, I could see there was something a little off about her face, a slight palsy on one side, and when she tried to walk her movements were slow and deliberate. Jake held her arm as if she were made of glass. For a moment, I considered hugging her; I felt like I knew her so well. But I hesitated. What did she remember? Maybe nothing at all.

"Madeline!" my father said as he walked towards her. "How wonderful to see you! Mia, go to the house and get your mother."

For a moment, I couldn't move. I looked at Mrs. Gerber-Starr, waiting for her to say something to me, to smile at least, but she didn't. She barely glanced at me. Then I looked at Rob. He sat there, in the driver's seat, staring straight ahead.

"Mia?" my father said again.

I took a breath and ran to the house.

In less than a minute I was following my mother across the front lawn as she rushed to embrace her friend. When she pulled back, she had tears in her eyes, but Mrs. G-S seemed strangely cool.

And when my mother insisted they come inside, Mrs. G-S begged off.

"Really, we can't stay," she said, forming the words slowly. "I just got home yesterday," she continued, "and I couldn't wait another minute to have my Rachel home with me." She paused. "Bill and I are so very grateful for all you've done."

"Of course," my mother replied, but I sensed the air shift. Things were suddenly awkward. It wasn't until Jake and I went inside to get Rachel's things that I realized what was happening. Madeline Gerber-Starr had come to collect her daughter. She didn't want Rachel in our house – my house – the house of the drunken internet slut and her terrible parents. Could this thing get any worse, you wonder? Oh yes…yes it could.

"How are you?" Jake asked as we filled Rachel's suitcase with clothes. I was so caught in my own thoughts about Rob and Mrs. G-S that I barely registered the question.

"I don't know," I answered irritably.

"Yeah, well, you were pretty messed up the last time I saw you."

"Those pictures are lies," I said angrily.

"I know," he said matter-of-factly. "I'm not talking about the pictures. I'm talking about the night of the party." He shook his head. "Shit, I had to actually carry you to the car."

WAIT. WHAT????

It was Jake? Jake who carried me? Jake who tried to button my shirt for me? Jake who'd dropped me on the doorstep? I opened my mouth to speak but he beat me to it.

"I'm really sorry I left you at the door like that," he said, reading the expression on my face. "I know it was an asshole move but I had basically stolen my dad's car to come get you, so I couldn't let your dad know it was me or he'd want to know how I got you home."

My memory goes sort of blank at this point. I don't know how I responded to him. I'm not even sure what happened next. Somehow, Jake got Rachel and most of her stuff out of the house and into the car. Somehow, I managed to *not* go outside again even though every cell in my body wanted to run to the car and bang on the windshield – to scream or cry or take my clothes off – anything to get Rob to see me, to notice me, to care.

Ellsworth High School Case #1141
Transcript of interview: March 23
Student: Mia Morgan
Counselor: Dr. Janis Dubrovski

Dr. Dubrovski: *I don't know where to go from here Mia. I'm sorry this happened to you, but without you sharing more, there is very little I can do to help you.*

Mia Morgan: *Yeah. Sure. I know.*

Dr. Dubrovski: *And you honestly have no intention of acting on any of this, in any way?*

Mia Morgan: *I'm not going to kill myself or anyone else if that's what you mean.*

CHAPTER 39

Life Savers

March 23rd

Another two weeks passed and slowly the kids in school were shifting back to their own lives. They ignored me but at least the taunts and wisecracks had died down. The Baditudes, however, weren't done. A new nail-polished slur appeared on my locker as quickly as I could get the previous one off, and whenever I walked by one of them, they coughed the word slut or bitch into their fists.

My mother took me shopping that Sunday to "celebrate" the end of my being grounded – not much to celebrate considering I had nowhere to go and no one to go with. It wasn't something she would ordinarily do but I could tell she felt sorry for me. The mall was about twenty minutes from our house, and we rode the first ten in silence. Finally, she said. "Are you ever going to tell me what's really going on?" And totally unexpectedly, I burst into tears.

We arrived at the mall a few minutes later and we sat in the parking lot while I cried. Then, I told her. I told her everything. The Rob stuff and the sex stuff and the Chloe stuff and the drinking and when I was done, she sighed and patted my hand. "Thank you for telling me," she said.

"You won't say anything, will you?"

She frowned. "Some of these kids deserve to be seriously punished, Mia."

I nodded. "I know. But that would just start the whole thing all over again and I don't think I can take it. Besides, I put myself in most of those situations by choice. And there was no permanent damage done – no one actually got hurt."

My mother shook her head. "Except Eric and the groundskeeper at Port Windsor and you, Mia. You got hurt."

"Yeah, I did. But I still don't want you to say anything." I looked at her beseechingly. "Promise you won't. It will just make it worse. You can't say anything. And you can't tell Dad. Please."

"You have my word. Under one condition."

I looked at her expectantly.

"We go in the mall and get you some *different* clothes."

I looked down at my tacky Baditude shirt and almost laughed. "Fine but I want to look normal, and not like I'm still in middle school."

"Deal." She smiled. Then she said. "I love you, Mia. I'm so sorry you went through all of this for so long all by yourself. But I'm here for you and this all will pass in time – maybe even faster than you think. You're just the most interesting thing happening right now – like Madeline's accident. It was the most important thing in the world until it wasn't – until something else happened. And while what happened to you was a doozy, as soon as the next scandal comes along, you will be yesterday's news."

I nodded, and my eyes filled with tears because for the first time in I don't know how long, I felt I had at least one friend in the world.

I had trouble sleeping that night. No surprise. The next day was Monday and I had to face it all again. But that night, for the first time since the night of the party, it wasn't self-pity or longing for Rob that kept me awake. It was anger – anger at Chloe and Kendal and Justin and Mike and all the rest of the kids who were so afraid to be imperfect or real or honest or weird that they ended up being cruel and ugly and even dangerous.

And Rob. Yes, FINALLY. I was angry at Rob. For being so incredibly selfish. SO. INCREDIBLY. SELFISH. I finally understood that the only person he cared about – really, genuinely cared about – was himself. Only his feelings counted. Only his needs mattered. Not Chloe's or even his mom's. And certainly not mine.

But even more than Rob – I was angry at Mrs. Gerber-Starr. How could she be so small and ungrateful – so worried about how things appeared that she'd turn her back on my mother after all my mother had done for her?

I woke up the next morning still tired, or maybe just weary. I was tired of being scared and sad and angry. Tired of trying – trying to look the way I thought Rob wanted me to look – trying to be something or someone that I didn't even really like. I wore the new jeans my mom had gotten me at the mall and an old Beatles t-shirt I'd bought at a garage sale a couple of years ago. I let my hair air dry (for the first time in forever) except with some new products I'd discovered to smooth the frizz and put on some mascara. The result was okay – not Baditude-worthy – but not a total loser either.

I took a deep breath and swallowed the dread in the back of my throat. It was going to be another long week.

My mother was in the kitchen when I got downstairs. "You better get a move on," she said, "You don't want to keep your friends waiting."

I looked at her like she was crazy.

"I hope you don't mind," she said. "I made a few calls."

I still didn't know what she was talking about but as I stepped outside, my heart jumped a beat. Angelica and Stephanie were standing at the end of my path. I walked towards them tentatively.

"Hey," Angelica said in greeting.

"What? No bagel?" Stephanie asked as if no time had gone by.

I shook my head. There was no way I could speak without crying.

Angelica rummaged through her backpack pocket. "You want a Life Saver?" she asked

I nodded. I never wanted a Life Saver so much in my life.

Epilogue

Almost a year has passed since the whole Rob Starr thing and some days it seems like maybe it never happened. My friends and I are good – tighter than ever – after we talked it all out. They explained that at first, they were just mad and hurt. I had blatantly broken our pact. So, together, they agreed to shut me out. But they never really meant for the fight to go on as long as it had. After three weeks of seeing me looking completely pathetic, they decided to forgive me. That same day, however, as fate would have it, Samantha saw me leaving school with Casey and Chloe; and well, after that (and the incident at the pizzeria) they just figured I didn't want them around. After a lot of tears (mostly mine), a heartfelt apology (from me), another heartfelt apology (from them) and the promise to never let a boy get in the way of our friendship again, we got back to being us.

We (my friends and I) are a lot less nerdy now. I mean we're not popular – not in a mainstream way anyway. But we've cultivated a sort of geeky/cool thing – you know vintage clothes, big glasses, so at least we've got some style. Some people even named us; WTF, like we're a clique or something. But we're not into that. We try to be nice to everyone.

Last week, Jake Starr asked me to the junior prom. Super weird, right? He's really kinda hot now, by the way. He grew another inch over the summer, and he's got this goofy-sweet, one-dimple smile that's just stupid cute. I guess I never noticed it because of how bad things were last year. He's been smiling a lot more since his parents got separated, though. I think it's been good for him.

I see him a lot since he sits next to me in Art. Turns out he wasn't just showing up for an easy A. He's really good, especially at drawing; maybe the best in the class. In fact, I'm pretty sure I misjudged him on a lot of things. Still, I had to say no to the prom thing. It's just too soon, and way too strange. Maybe. Someday.

● ● ●

The Baditudes broke up last summer. Something about Kendal and Luke (Casey's boyfriend). But it was bound to happen regardless of the circumstances – they were just too nasty to last. And anyway, most of them were off to college, busy trying to figure out what came next in their lives; high school suddenly seeming small and insignificant in the rear-view mirror.

It would be great if I could tell you that Rob and Chloe and Kendal and Justin and Mike and Reynolds and Candie all got what they deserved, but they didn't. Rob was playing basketball at Babson, one of the best Division Three schools in the country. Apparently if you're a good athlete and your dad's rich, colleges are welcoming regardless of your Trig grades.

Kendal was at one of the so-so SUNY schools. Justin and Mike were both at West Virginia which they chose solely based on it being ranked the biggest party school in America the prior year. Reynolds was at Vanderbilt, where his dad was a legacy, and Candie was at Princeton. Chloe got a full ride for cheerleading at the University of South Carolina, but I heard she was trying to transfer somewhere closer to Rob. It might have just been a rumor, but no one would be surprised if it were true. It never occurred to me back then, but now I realize she's probably as ORD about Rob as I was.

Mrs. Gerber-Starr still has a hint of a limp and the tiniest droop near her left eye but overall, her recovery was pretty miraculous.

And, now that Mr. Starr is living with some other woman, Mrs. G-S has become a much nicer, humbler person. She apologized to my mother. I guess being dumped on her ass by her douche of a husband helped her figure out a few things. Public humiliation is a great teacher. Take it from me.

I am still a bit broken – okay, maybe a lot broken. I have bad days. Days when I find myself wondering what would have happened if Rob had hit that foul shot. And I get sad, as if I was somehow robbed of a happy ending by the laws of physics and gravity. As if Rob making that shot would have made Rob the guy he pretended to be. As if Rob Starr and Mia Morgan were ever really possible.

And then there are the days when I go to school and someone makes a joke or a snide comment about those pictures, or some delusional asshole hits on me, thinking that I might really be what those kids said I was. And I get mad. Really, really mad.

In therapy I talk about what happened. I try to forgive Justin and Mike and Kendal and Chloe and all the Baditudes for what they did – if only so I can move forward – but it's hard to find an excuse for their behavior. And there are a lot of days when I regret that they didn't face any consequences for their actions. But back when it first happened – when Dr. Dubrovski was questioning me – I was too scared to tell the truth; still too involved, still hoping it was all some kind of mistake.

And I know, no matter how much therapy I have, I will never forgive Rob. He used me and lied to me and manipulated me because that's who he really is, a user and a liar and a manipulator. And because the only thing that matters to Rob Starr is Rob Starr.

I still have that video on my phone. You remember – the one Rob made in the parking lot of the school where he professed his love for me at the top of his lungs. And I watch it sometimes. And sometimes, on the bad days, I even think of posting it because, you know, fuck him.

But as mad as I am at him, I've also learned that the person I'm most mad at is me. How could I have let all those things happen? And, okay, most of what happened wasn't my fault; but some of it was – a lot of it was. I was the one who pretended to be something I wasn't, who was convinced I wasn't good enough the way that I was. Rob never asked for me to change myself – not really. He never specifically said, wear shorter skirts or blow dry your hair every day or put on more makeup. He never told me to listen to crappy pop music or explicitly insist that I drink or have sex with him. He just liked me better when I wasn't me. Which means he never really liked me – Mia Morgan – at all. And the truth is – I knew it – I knew it the entire time. But I kept lying to myself – kept trying to make him love me – giving away pieces of myself with every compromise.

And maybe worst realization of all was that I didn't really like him either. I mean sure, I liked who he was and how he looked, but we were never really friends. I invented that just like I invented everything else. When we talked it was him talking – about basketball or his mom or his dad or his grades. I can't remember a time when he asked me a single thing about me. And did I mention he had THE worst taste in music? Seriously.

But most of the time, I'm happier on the days that I don't think about it at all. And there are more and more of those days with each passing week.

Lately I've been trying to figure out what I might want to study when it's my turn to go to college. I'm thinking about becoming a recovery therapist or maybe even a doctor. The stuff I learned at the hospital when Mrs. G-S was sick was kind of awesome. I know becoming a doctor is really hard – there's a lot of studying and science and stuff – but you know, the truth is, I'm pretty damn good at that stuff. I am a mathlete after all.

The best days are the ones when I can see how lucky I am. Sure, I went through something awful, but it could have been worse. I survived. And I have real friends who are funny and smart and care about me.

And I have me.

The real me.

And I'll never give myself away to someone who doesn't deserve me again.

About the Author

J. A. Howard (aka Julie Howard) is a lifelong reader, lover and writer of YA, fantasy, and science fiction. She is also a strategy and branding consultant in New York. The mother of two daughters, she is a strong advocate for the healthy development and empowerment of women and girls. Julie lives with her family and their two German Shorthaired Pointers, Bo and Otis.

You can find more about Julie on her website jahoward.com

www.ingramcontent.com/pod-product-compliance
Lightning Source LLC
Chambersburg PA
CBHW050732180626
46814CB00002B/726